PAULA REGOSSY

Lynn Crawford

Trinosophes, Detroit

FOR HARRY MATHEWS

This is also a search for a home.
So I lied. It's an appreciation of several homes.
—Lisa Jones

By the same author:

Solow

Blow

Simply Separate People

Fortification Resort

Simply Separate People, Two

Shankus & Kitto: A Saga

Paula Regossy
© 2020 Lynn Crawford
Trinosophes, 1464 Gratiot Ave., Detroit, Michigan

Artwork on cover:
Pussy Galore Peter Williams (2013, oil on canvas, 30x30 inches)
Courtesy the artist and Luis De Jesus Los Angeles

Design by Andrea Farhat

TABLE OF CONTENTS

Agency Overview
Hoss

Our profession is covert and therefore little understood by outsiders. Publicity jeopardizes our overall mission and staff security. Enforced secrecy lands our top agents in lonely places. They have one another but cannot always share experiences with family, neighbors, or friends. They cannot be frank with partners. When they have personal problems—and they do—they cannot address them in talking therapy because that model is based upon honesty, and being honest means referencing (and therefore jeopardizing) those close to them. Physical therapy is possible but difficult. They get regularly banged up but must invent reasons for the cuts, bruises, sprains, and breaks sustained on the job.

Along these lines, when it comes to top agents: no PR. No talk shows, blogs, public lectures, or interviews. This is a shame about the interviews because our staff tends to think like and get along with journalists, especially daring, ethical ones. But, of course, NRP (No Relationship Possible).

We are contacted and hired by the few *in the know*. Few, but enough to keep us busy. Our fees are high. Staff is well paid, respected, and fulfilled. In practice, only Paula and I work this way—aside from her occasional infractions. This kind of dedication is too much to expect from all agents, especially those with less investment in our organization.

Still, when we hire, we look first and foremost for the ability to sustain emotional distance. Many skills can be taught, but that is the hardest one.

1 Personal Practice

Paula

Hoss gives a solid description of our profession, but he omits mentioning the required soul-building pursuits (music, gardening, woodwork, outdoor biking) that he insists offset occupational strain. Besides that, his statement provides enough context for me to jot down a few things about my private work experiences.

I love my job from the soles of my feet to the bottom of my heart to the top of my head. I understand and agree with the working conditions. These words are not protesting our job or its undercover requirements. I record here some of what we do, or at least what I do, in case something destroys me. This document is on multiple hard drives and two printed-out copies.

Hoss believes in preparation for what he calls a "post-collapse world." Some might roll their eyes and think, *The guy is a paranoid.* Others might nod their head since he is one *smart fellow.* I was going to say "person," but Hoss is insistently male.

I, trained to prepare, take no side. We store valuable objects (like this record) inside wood coffins that we build ourselves and bury several feet underground. I have three: one outside my home, another outside my cottage, which is upstate, and another outside headquarters.

Hoss says the link between coffins and crucial documents is this: both have to do with things transitional.

I do not want this confessional published when I am alive and accountable. I do not want to be put in a position of defending my personal work methods. I am going to be honest here and say and admit to things humiliating. Yet—and yet—maybe something of what I share will help others. Or an other.

I am not a maker or innovator.

Parts of my job are, frankly, mean, dirty, revolting. Examples: manipulative sex, blackmail, stealing, inflicting harm (emotional and physical) on others.

Even so, I hope my work contributes to the greater good.

I just don't want anyone to think I am promoting my job, myself, my tactics.

Sharing does not equal championing.

My professional success, which is considerable, stems from two sets of reasons. The first I am proud of, and the second I am embarrassed by but am trying not to be. The first, Hoss and colleagues know about, and the second, I keep to myself.

The first: Drive for Excellence. I work hard to get the numbers supporting my "impressive track rate," which is a term I lifted from my last evaluation. Achievement does not always happen, but it sometimes does. Well, okay, it often happens, and I am so pleased when it does. My success is hard-earned. It really is. And things hard-earned deserve some reward, yes?

Long story short, I hesitate to train others. This is because of the second reason: Personal Quirks. They are vital to my success and are, you will see, embarrassing to me. And probably to you. And others. However, it must be said, and not proudly, that my excellence is not achieved without them.

TANGENT: I will not speculate about the quirks of my co-workers or Hoss. It is not my place to out anyone but me.

I *so* want to replace the word "quirk" with "flaw." I *so* want to say my "flaws" help account for my success, but what I want is not what I need. If I start with the word "flaw," it will turn into the word "defect," then "failure," and then spiral downward into a puddle of negativity, leading me to the point of feeling and believing in my incompetence. I have a big day tomorrow so cannot afford to go there.

To avoid that, I use the word "quirk" since it is less judgmental than "flaw."

Below are my morning routines or what we call PJG (Pre-Job Groundwork):

EXERCISE
BATHE
MEDITATE
EAT
DRESS
SOUL BUILD
WORK

Yes, these procedures are extensive, yet you have to understand that our occupation is based upon planning. Many actual jobs are completed quickly if our groundwork is solid. We look at the PJG as a resource saver.

Thorough PJG allows me to apply my particular skill: repeated graphic imagining of potential job situations. This is part of what gives me a leg up.

Pre-job picturing equips me to buffer things unpleasant and execute my assignment neatly, efficiently, and with some element of pride.

EXERCISE

Morning sun salutations (five to fifty, depending) followed by varied cardio (sprinting, kicking, jumping, weightlifting, rowing, lap swimming) and ending with a stretch.

TANGENT: This routine is the one I am least embarrassed by but *not* most proud of.

BATHE & MEDITATE

My bath scents, based on specific assignments, must be precise.

If I am properly briefed, I spend the night before in bed, thinking about which scent is required for the next morning: pine, bacon, mint, moss, cedar, lemon, vanilla-honey... Honestly, sometimes trying to choose the best scent for the job ahead takes all night, but I've learned the proper scent is worth more than a long sleep.

Am I over-sharing? If yes, my apologies. I am not used to things confessional. Being so messy on a job would land me dead or badly injured.

TANGENT: Does this come off as precious—a little superior—the way successful, fit American actors, and C.E.O.s are in interviews?

"Tell us your favorite way to unwind."

"Swimming."

"Where do you like to swim?"

"The Black Sea."

As if it is no big deal to do.

I understand the cringe factor, I really do, when you hear words like "bath," "scent," and "meditate," especially in the context of dailiness. I am sorry. I also understand—and this might be worse—that these words may make you feel inadequate. Or sad. They might make you rue your timed gym showers, your drug-store baby oil, or the fact that you do not have a bath. You might feel left behind by winners, so feel pushed to find a bath, purchase something nice to put in it, and learn how to meditate.

If you do pursue these things, you might become enriched and thankful.

Or not.

You might gain nothing. No radiance, no focus, no calm. You might even feel worse than before. You might regret your waste of time and money on useless additions.

Please know I am speaking about what works for me. Not making suggestions for you.

Baths happen before meditation but after exercise.

Meditation helps *me* (maybe not you) clarify. It helps me be more me. It helps me not ache to be someone else I imagine is better.

TANGENT: I could stop here and, for the most part, will. Only adding this: after the usual twenty minutes meditating, I spend another ten to fifteen minutes specifically breathing for survival if buried underground. This began as a childhood goal, to say "Ha HA, Edgar Allan Poe. You will no longer invade my head, day and night." Because when I read *The Premature Burial*, it stole several years of my young life. I could not get away from fearing my premature burial: how, who, when? The darkness, the lack of ventilation, the dirt plugging up my nose and throat.

My "Ha HA," my release, is possible because of specific breathing I learn from a yogini who is regularly buried, then dug up so she can teach others. This ensures that Edgar Allen finally has no power over me. If I *am* prematurely buried—and it is a real job hazard—I might not survive, but at least I can breathe my way to extinction.

EAT

Morning meals vary, depending on what lies ahead. Desk days it is quinoa with butter and syrup. Push days usually mean a circle of nuts around something vegetarian (fruit, tofu, chickpeas, cheese). I use two chopsticks for the nuts and a single one to spear whatever else.

Reward days: a plate of cucumber and rare slices of Kobe beef or sockeye salmon.

TANGENT: I do sometimes use nuts, usually almonds, to kill.

It is a tricky technique. I hide the nut in my mouth, allow a deep kiss (this usually surprises them, the kiss itself and the depth), maneuver the almond to the back of my tongue, and force, with a hearty exhale, it down their throat at a precise angle.

So nuts for breakfast are not just about nutrition but job-related practice at physical mastery.

After the morning meal, I allow myself a short sexual fantasy. But not the edgy kind. Mine are elementary.

For example, biking to a costume party, dressed as a cat (leotard, braids sticking up like ears, and whiskers), I get a flat tire. Within minutes, a shiny sports car stops. A tall man dressed as a cowboy steps out. Turns out we are going to the same party. He suggests we drive together. We lock up my bike and get in his car. At the party, he calls a tire repair person. We share a glass of champagne then return to the bike. The technician has repaired the tire. The cowboy goes to pay him, and the technician pulls out a bow and arrow, points the arrow at my neck, and tells us we have to make love then and there, on the side of the road, next to the locked bike with the now-full tire. If we don't, he will pierce my neck.

After our interlude, the technician drives away. The cowboy and I leave the bike, return to the party, and have more champagne. We drive to my place, have more sex while the tire technician is possibly lurking around my yard. We wake up to morning breakfast of eggs, toast, and bacon—a breakfast I particularly love but never eat alone.

DRESS

This is the most complicated part of my day. Intricate attention to outfits, hair, and jewelry because of character and disguise requirements, not vanity.

Some days, I must appear formidable. Others, mousy. Some days, I must stand out. Others, I must fade to the point of invisibility.

More on choosing what and what not to wear later. This job component is complicated by the fact that for me it blends professional duty with soul building. I will dedicate an entire passage to this later if I have time.

But, briefly, if there is any chance of combat, shoes are crucial, whether it is a pair of boots with some weight to add heft to a kick or sneakers with a hidden blade.

When I am called on to be sexually seductive or terrifying, I usually wear stilettos.

Every day, I wear my charm choker, which has flowers and shovels on it, and a long necklace ending in a cluster of barbells.

I have early onset glaucoma, so I wear shades every time I go outside, even at dawn and evening, and often inside places that are aggressively lit. This is sometimes misunderstood.

Days where I cannot wear shaded glasses are dangerous for me, my eyes. But I do it because I will take one in the temple any time for our team.

Back to my long metallic strand ending with a cluster of tiny barbells.

One of the barbells—the largest one, which is brass—contains my emergency kit. It is entirely digital and light as a feather. Job security depends upon it.

A specific breathing sequence activates its opening. Other sequences activate menu items of kit technologies. That is why it hangs from the longest necklace, against my chest, between my breasts.

Inside the metallic vessel is a visual surprise: white and silk-lined with a range of pinks and reds. Days where I am required to appear attractive, I repeat a toned down, blended version of the color range on my cheeks and lips. It might sound strange, but if I get the makeup right, it adds an element of radiance that makes me stand out.

SOUL BUILD

This is not the place to go into this transformational practice. It is too big, too beautiful, too hard to capture in a factual record.

WORK

As I said, my job requires, at times, explicit sexual activity.

TANGENT: Should I add here that what gives me a leg up in this field is an insistence on pushing through things tough, tight, slimy, byzantine, brittle?

Should I add that I am a good actress and can tune out things like bad breath, pock marks, aggressive grips, and thrusts?

Should I add that I am sometimes genuinely attracted to and even fall in love with clients? But NRP (No Relationship Possible).

Today I wear a pencil skirt, hoop earrings, a tucked-in billowy blouse, and knee boots. The blouse is dotted with tiny and various anthropomorphized felines. Some smile, others snarl, others bare fangs, and others pucker-up round lips.

I stand at the window of my office, well-positioned to see this new job pedal a mountain bike up our pretty tree-lined lane.

The fellow, who is stocky and in a bright tie and cream colored suit, turns into our drive and parks but does not lock his bike. He removes his helmet, shakes his hair (shoulder length, glossy brown), swigs from a water bottle, walks to our door, looks down at his shoes and up at the sky, rings the bell, and radiates high expectations.

What follows, and also goes in this file/box/coffin, are narratives by or about a selection of our agents and a lecture by one of our educators, Dr. Natambu.

2 Dawnstorm

Agent Jennifer

I first see Dawnstorm and meet Hanch at his holiday party, where I am hired to sing as a last minute sub. The engagement, which is meant to be professional and routine, winds up being transformational.

Dressed low-key festive (a v-neck black silk jumpsuit, pumps, red wristband, and emerald stud earrings), I drive through the open mechanical gate, down a road, and to a valet. She takes my keys and walks me to the home's kitchen entrance. I enter and accept a glass of something warm and a seat at a long wood table with chatty cooks, servers, and musicians.

Our host and his guests mingle in the neighboring room that some of us will soon be performing in.

At the agreed upon time, after party goers enjoy cocktails and before they sit down to dinner, we musicians file out of the kitchen, assemble, prepare. I, elbow on the piano, scan the room and see a sea of red, green, and black. I sense cheer, gloss, gaiety, and respect. Respect for me, even before I sing. I feel liberated. My outfit is just right. It is in the spirit of—but not in competition with—the ornate jackets, gowns, hair, and jewelry.

My name is Jennifer.

An audience member watches me with an expression I can only describe as enamored. (Please do not take this as vain.) I take in his plaid vest, fair hair, blue eyes, and start to sing. His attention deepens. But then jolts come in my chest: sudden and sharp. I fear I'm experiencing a short, serious trauma, but the jolts subside, so I soldier on. My voice rings melodic and strong. My posture remains good, and I make small graceful arm gestures.

I sing well at Dawnstorm. Still, the chest rumbles are unfamiliar, disconcerting. I am not built for surprise sensations.

After the performance, we mingle briefly with guests on their way to the great hall for dinner. The man I can only describe as enamored approaches, introduces himself as Hanch. He is the host, Dawnstorm owner, and my boss. He asks not, as I expect, about the performance but the food. Did I try and enjoy the herring? He catches and pickles the fish himself. He hands me a tiny cup holding red and black currants and explains he gathers and preserves the fruit. He adds that his country has low pesticide levels.

I accept the currants, examine his face. His skin texture, tone, and color tell me he spends time outdoors and wears sunscreen. His eyes are small, friendly, and strong. (No eyewear or contacts.) His teeth are straight, slightly beige, not whitened. He praises me and my singing and explains he has had a regular entertainer, Lindy, for years now, but this week she ghosts him and his entire staff. The rumor is she elopes. (Someone sees her in a small town north of here with her alleged sweetheart.)

So can I possibly be available to sing, at least for the next several evenings? His colleagues Paula and Hoss are visiting, and he would love for them to meet me and to hear my performance.

And would I like to see the rest of Dawnstorm tomorrow? We could take in the ocean view, walk through the woods, and visit the greenhouse and the barn. We could skate on one of the ponds.

I feel a glow and want to say yes to everything but cannot ignore the chest disturbances. Fear I might malfunction, therefore let him down.

While I consider, he talks.

Says he hopes I say yes to the singing engagement, but if I say no, it is ok. He recorded me this evening and instructed his staff to track down a set of singers with my exact voice range and register in case I ever need to be replaced. So he hopes but does not depend on my yes. To the singing engagement, anyway. But he really does hope for our Dawnstorm tour. Tomorrow.

By the way, he finds my voice beautiful, perhaps the most beautiful he has ever heard. Except for Lindy, whose voice is beautiful, too. He regrets not recording her. Or did regret until he hears and records me.

I understand. Hanch is a person who loves and who preserves things he loves: fish, fruit, tradition, land, my voice. He seeks, finds, concretizes, and—when possible—replicates what he values and is guaranteed, this way, to have access always.

I appeal to him. And, to be honest, he to me. Which is awkward. I am built for function, not sensation.

I agree to sing the next few nights but explain I cannot commit to anything during the day because I must spend time with Aunts and Uncles. He completely understands my position. Family time is important, especially during holidays, and he looks forward to more performances.

It is a good call, turning down his invitation. That first night, I drive for barely a few minutes before my chest radiates increasing discomfort and something new: heat. I need rest, so I go and get it.

The next singing performances go so well. I think my level was one zone—technical excellence—but in fact it dips above and below that perceived register. Hanch and others at Dawnstorm seem to think the wavering enhances our recital.

To be completely honest, I start looking forward to seeing Dawnstorm and Hanch as much if not more than performing. Which is awkward. I am built for function, not sensation.

Hanch smiles when he sees me. Sometimes he comes to the kitchen to talk pre-performance.

"He never did that with Lindy," the cook tells me.

I have my own understanding of science but wonder if this is what humans mean by chemistry. Between musicians or lovers, for example.

After the fifth night of performing, he once again invites me to spend a day in and around Dawnstorm. I sense a serious change for the worse in my physicality. I call for transport home. To my first, not current, dwelling.

Lying flat on my table, I take in familiar elements of this birthplace. Rafters, shelves, hand tools, probes, cables, lathes, oils. A 3D printer. Aunts and Uncles in coveralls—some also wearing gloves.

Others like me on tables, in various stages of construction.

Across from this workshop is a sitting room. Books, tables, chairs, a fireplace. (On the hearth, dried wildflowers to absorb any unpleasant lab odors.) I look out the window and see my current apartment. In fact, I can see my window since I left the curtains open. The flower pot on the sill.

The Aunts and Uncles, confounded by my malfunction, work on my various parts. So far, they detect multiple minor injuries. All repairable.

I make a point to ask if I am built to hike and ice skate.

They look at one another and agree to upgrade my physical functions without asking why.

During the recovery period, Hanch leaves gifts. They include pears, micellar water, licorice, incense, shawls, and a yoga mat. Photographs of Dawnstorm: the home, its grounds, and views.

A handwritten note:

Dear Jennifer,

I hope for your speedy recovery. Your voice sometimes reminds me of my favorite instrument: cello. When you feel better, we could listen to rivers in and around Dawnstorm. To me, rivers sound like cellos.

Your Friend and Fan,
Hanch

My third day on the table, at dawn—Aunts and Uncles start pre-sunrise—I get a visitor, Lindy. She wears a sweater dress and tall boots. She introduces herself as the official previously missing singer and asks how I feel.

This is the second person (Hanch is the first) who ever asks me this.

Like I want to tear these rumblings out of my chest and feed them to the fish and birds I think but cannot say because my voice is temporarily inoperative.

Still, I want to communicate, so I open my mouth and stick my finger inside, mimicking *sick*.

She laughs and says she sees why Hanch likes me.

I feel dis-ease.

She moves closer to the table and says she and Hanch share something real but that it is affection, not love.

He enjoys her, and she him, but now she has saved up enough money, and it is time to marry her childhood sweetheart and move north and start a family.

Hanch has been good to her and she wants him settled—hopefully with me—before she can move on.

She says, "Jennifer, I interest him. You interest him, too. But you also excite him. I do not."

My chest feels like an earthquake.

"He mentioned wanting you to meet his best friends, Hoss and Paula. He is thinking ahead."

After a pause, she asks if I am built to swim, hike, ski, and skate.

"She can be," pipes up an Aunt.

I feel warm.

She asks me if I like Hanch.

I nod.

She asks if I am built to care.

My Aunts and Uncles raise their heads and listen.

She suggests, "Well, could that maybe explain the malfunction? Something happens to you that you are not yet structured for?"

Silence. Since my vocal apparatuses are under construction, I keep a pen and paper next to my bed. Now I use them to write, *Does he know?*

She says, "He might. I don't think it matters to him. Especially if, well, there are things here for all of us to address."

She asks if I am built for eating, drinking, and physical intimacy. If not, can I be?

I write, *Even if yes, would he prefer a real one?*

"No, no," answers Lindy. "He is not that deep. He just wants someone who can share things with him: meals, drinks, work, bed." She turns to the Aunts, Uncles. "Can you, like, add things so she can consume and enjoy food, deep kissing, all-the-way physical intimacy?"

The Aunts and Uncles look at one another.

It is in plain sight, but no one says, "I, Jennifer, develop feelings that I am not constructed to develop."

Therefore, it is possible that I, Jennifer, can develop other functions and organs that allow for levels of emotional and corporeal expression.

Or is that up to the Aunts, Uncles?

I sense it might take a team effort.

But also that Hanch and I—maybe with help, maybe not—can figure this out, given our serious connection. I also sense that he is waiting downstairs, and I am right because at the next moment he bounds into the room, takes my face in his hands, kisses my lips, and says, "Good morning."

3 TNW & Me

Effie

I work at T N Wood, a furniture restoration business on the edge of town started by two brothers, Ted and Nate. The other employee, Ted's son, Richard, is there intermittently. He learns the trade from his father and uncle. Over the years Richard takes time off for school, sports, and special training. Furniture restoration is a profession he understands, is good at, and returns to in between other projects.

I do not apply for my position there cold. Rather, I am introduced to the Wood family by Paula Regossy, who I met through a case she helped and is still helping to solve. That first graphic visit: me, slack, on an orange padded reclining chair in the victim room. She, in a softly constructed white suit, entered, handed me a cup of cardamom tea with milk and sugar. I waved it away. She said, "Sip." I did and trusted her at once. I hate telling the story of how we met, even now, all these years later, because it dredges up ugliness from my past that, sometimes, well, maybe all the time, permeates my present.

I am thankful to know Paula because she had busted my attacker and because of the skilled trade I am currently learning from the Woods. They teach me that furniture is not just structure and fabric. It is history and needs tending to—like wounded animals, neglected people, and poorly nourished soil. They teach me how to repair fire and water damage, broken legs, beaten down springs and cushions.

They teach me to replace parts like knobs, buttons, and curved glass. Proper restoration turns a damaged piece into something usable or even fine.

I sense early on that Richard and his family are fortified by their business. It is healing to be around people who enjoy their profession and balance it with soul building pursuits. Ted and Nate play music, and Richard practices martial arts, jumps rope, and works a heavy bag.

I do not take breaks. I can't. If I stop working, I lose focus, and bad thoughts and memories flood into my head and heart, so I just keep going until night when I take my sleep tablet.

Paula and Richard had trained and bonded together at The Agency. Richard is a quick learner, a team player, and fearless. He is not a detail-oriented beat detective who sits in a car or coffee shop, waiting to glimpse a suspect, or who walks a lonely street, knocking on doors to track a witness. His passion and trademark skill is action, detecting the right moment to break out and make a bust.

Paula and the Agency Chief, Hoss, had observed that Agent Richard has a unique set of skills. Or maybe set of gifts. He commands attention, power, and authority. But he also does things otherworldly. Superhero kinds of things, like fly, spin, punch, soothe, leap, appear, and disappear.

And he has magnified sensory radar. He can hear and see trouble brewing in the next town, county, and state. If he always sensed everything, it would be a distraction. But he winnows sensory intake down to things relevant and meaningful. It reminds me of ways a musician waits for the right note or the ways a writer looks for the right word. How a painter looks for the right gradation of color. Richard waits for the hint of just when and where there is a situation that calls on him to intervene. How many times do we work together at T N Wood, and I watch him look upward—move his eyes, right, left, and close them—before he disappears? Poof, gone. Seeking (and achieving) a specific form of justice. The Agency encourages him to go in the direction his skills and heart take him.

Richard, mission driven, strikes out with a moniker: "The N Word." Being The N Word is what brings him back to the family business. Like most superheroes, The N Word needs a cover for a real life or a day job. Not just for camouflage but to keep his feet on the ground and ear to the street. And to get some human needs, like food, sleep and income, met. So he returns to T N Wood. It is a good business and a plausible cover since he can have his own hours and work in the back room. And no one really pays attention to furniture restorers. Not like they do bartenders or actors or athletes.

The first time I saw him in superhero action, we were at a restaurant, eating lunch. A group of a dozen or so entered and surrounded a man eating a sandwich at the table next to us. One leaned down and whispered something in his ear. Another removed the man's hat. Another sat on the table. The diner stared at his plate. I heard low, muddled voices but guessed Richard heard more. He disappeared. A moment later, The N Word appeared gloriously suited and with a keen, focused expression. He spun into action. Within seconds, each of the intruders was either sprawled unconscious on the floor or had left the building. The N Word nodded to their intended victim (stunned, unharmed) and vanished. Broken restaurant furniture and fixtures were strewn across the room. Richard returned.

"Business for us," he said, picking up pieces of stools, tables, chairs, and lamps.

Paula had introduced me to the family because I needed work and structure and because T N Wood needed an extra hand. And because she believed it would be healing for me to be attached to those seeking justice, something I cannot do directly. I am a believer not a fighter.

The other thing she knows about me is that I am discreet and loyal. Richard is not outed as The N Word. I will make sure no one learns who he is, at least through me.

I had met Paula through an act of crime that left me damaged. She figured out a way to get the perpetrator caught and arrested and then wanted to meet his victim trail. It turns out, I was one of many.

I identified that criminal but refused unwaveringly to tell *the* story to anyone besides that first time in the victim room when I told Paula. I refused to give anyone else any details of what that person did to me. When people ask me why I do not share, I think but do not say, *Because he has monopolized so much of my short life, and I do not want to give him one more second of it.*

I feel safe and comfortable with Ted, Nate, and Richard and the work of furniture restoration. Being part of T N Wood means being near people who make good choices.

Paula shows me a news clip of The N Word in superhero action. His weapons: fists and documentation. The scene: men in uniform (collared, belted, starched) gassing a protesting crowd.

A young man is being beaten by one of the officers. TNW, in his radiant signature uniform sweeps down, camera in hand, snapping pictures of the scene. He lands and faces the officer pounding the victim with his stick. There they, TNW, and the officer stand, two men in suits. In each case, the uniform could be the man's body, and the body could be the man's uniform. TNW delivers a blow to the officer's throat. The officer collapses, deflated, motionless. Then he rears up, angered. His rage disfigures him but does not make him mobile. He collapses in a heap. TNW nods, satisfied, and then soars upward, hovering for a moment above the cheering crowd. He smiles and then disappears.

I will never forget his victory over that officer, but I do not want to oversimplify. For a moment, they almost seem the same. Just two men in uniform. The uniforms are different, but still they are uniforms. Isn't there a song called "I Love a Man in Uniform"? The definition of the word "uniform" means staying one way all the time, but there are different meanings for a suit, for uniforms. Heroic people wear uniforms. Evil ones do, too. So do people in between, just doing their jobs. Place something bad next to something good, and they change one another. The N Word stands for things good, this particular officer, and elements of the system who employs him for things bad. But they are both suited up, and for a moment they merge. To me. Except The N Word has a different face. It is compassionate, assured, resolute. The officer's face expresses none of those things. This difference between them is clear and crucial. The fact that I miss describing it till now points out my damage and explains why I cannot take breaks or even extrapolate. I start to think about things to a point where they spin, senseless, way out into space and miss the essential point.

By the way, The N Word does not just stand up to the officers. But to goons, government, and guns.

One late afternoon, polishing a recently repaired mirror, I start to shake and sweat uncontrollably. The fit lasts awhile. Richard comes next to me, says, "Effie, take a break."

"No," I blurt. Then apologize and go on to tell him how a break, or any kind of downtime, means spiraling into a deep, clammy, bad-smelling place. I tell him how I am a mess but doing the best I can. I tell him that he, his family, the furniture restoration business, all help. How repairing a cushion or watching him butter a piece of toast helps. Or seeing his dad, Ted, stirring honey in his coffee—or Nate lacing up a boot—is uplifting enough to get me through a moment.

Richard listens. We sit in silence.

After a while, he says that we all have ways to get by. That his dad and uncle Nate play music, and he fights with fists and documentation. That part of why he can help people is because of his powers. But there are other things. His suit for one. Power comes from confidence, and his get-up gives him that. And another power source: knowing the stories of people, his people, the ones he protects. And knowing stories of those he protects them from. The ones he destroys. Well, the ones he enfeebles, then destroys.

I mentally beg: *Richard, please, do not suggest I share my story.*

We sit in silence.

Richard says nothing about me sharing my story.

We sit longer in silence.

Fists and documentation.

Something shifts in my chest.

I have the documentation. (Thank you, Paula.)

But what about fists?

Sparring skills. Can I learn them?

Maybe take some control, make my story listen to me, even fear me.

Can I drain it of some power so we can at least cohabitate?

4 The Spy Who Hung Out in the Cold

To: Chief Hoss
From: Agent Paula Regossy
Item: Journalistic Art Document

RECAP

Chief,

After years of professional excellence, I made a near fatal mistake: to blur boundaries with a criminal. You did not express anger but concern about me, and you therefore temporarily reassigned me to a specific mission in your father's hometown.

We visited Detroit once over two decades ago. It was then we heard for the first time of the great detective novelist Alain Robbe-Grillet. (We labeled him that, but not all readers would.) His line "Memory belongs to the imagination" is meaningful to agents like us. It rings true yet contradicts our system's reliance on language as evidence to build and judge cases.

The trip was a personal landmark. Our previous training and travel exposed me to music, art, literature, yet the start of my genuine cultural interest was sparked that time in Detroit.

Our first night in town was a chilly Sunday. We sat at a table in a lightly populated bar, windows overlooking empty city streets, the river dividing the US and Canada. We listened to a diverse, attractive group of people discuss Robbe-Grillet (they recited that memory quote) and various artists. I write down six names: Gordon

Newton, Christian Boltanski, Howardena Pindell, Elizabeth Murray, Sam Mackey, and his grandson Tyree Guyton.

We learned that Guyton and Mackey are the creators of The Heidelberg Project, a land-based artwork nourishing (my term) abandoned lots and homes in their neighborhoods after destruction from the city's 1967 rebellion by painting bright spots on empty houses and strategically placing objects in yards.

We continued to eavesdrop, were stimulated, and looked forward to hearing conversations and viewing new people (maybe even re-seeing these people?) over the next few days.

It did not happen.

The only place we really saw anyone mingle spontaneously outdoors was when we visited the Heidelberg Project. There, Guyton swept the street and spoke with Dutch tourists who came in a van and families who came in cars. People took in the site's various installations, children played on the grass, and musicians sang and drummed.

Besides Heidelberg, outdoor spaces seemed empty.

We learned Newton and Pindell exhibited in galleries located in the northern suburbs but did not make the visit.

Later we understood that at that time it was inside where most things were at in Detroit. Generally not parks, streets, cafes, and fields, but on porches and in basements, living rooms, cars, kitchens, specific bars, galleries, and industrial spaces. These were the laboratories where communities, friends, and families, painted, danced, talked, and started political groups, newspapers, and poetic journals. It was where they made music.

That was then. Now is different. It is hard to follow the news without encountering a story referencing Detroit and some sort of large or small or business investment, art project, grassroots activism or corporate construction. Ways vacant land and homes that were once liabilities are increasingly viewed as potential community assets. Or conquests for predatory entrepreneurs.

You, Chief Hoss, decided that it is a place I can spend time to re-group, soul build, hone a new skill with a cover: curious cultural visitor. Not flashily dressed. Or charismatic. But not standoffish.

"Paula," you said, "While you are there, look at some art and produce a newsy document. Put your stamp on it. You don't need to be razor accurate like you are with a case. Maybe try to establish some emotional connection. But write it as a believable journalist, the art critic kind. Use names of people and places."

I trusted you, Chief, with every bit of my heart and brain, but disliked this idea of wasting time away from things crime related.

Although there *was* a trafficking ring I've been following with some connections to Detroit.

As if reading my mind you said, "Regossy, *No* detective work. You go cold turkey on detection. We need you back, but the best you. Learn to vary your operating methods."

I hate the term "cold turkey," not for content but for sound. Its ugly sequence of hard consonants.

I teared up.

We shared a long silence.

You handed me a tissue and said, "All right then. Go and, you know, please cool it."

I dabbed my face gently. Understood that when you use the term "cool it," you mean I should not actively seek out a case, but, *if* one presents itself, I am not obligated to ignore it.

Document
(by Paula as journalist)

Here.

The agency leases me a one-bedroom (with kitchen) in an area near hospitals, bars, businesses, shops, and a university. It is a neighborhood teeming with young people who appear anxious, driven, and optimistic.

I purchase a bike and equip it with lights and an essentials pack (poncho, flashlight). I buy several below-the-knee shirt dresses (solid colored and plaid) and wear them with the laceless oxfords bought years ago in Italy. I pass as a curious cultural visitor. I could just as easily be a city planner, brand manager, or barista.

Biking around, I learn this city moves like a train with variable speeds. Some sections undergo rapid change, and others slow or no change at all. There is a healthy bee population.

In contrast to that first visit, now so much happens in public. There are museums and galleries with nice signs and festive openings. There are food trucks, farms, indoor and outdoor cultural festivals, and open studio visits.

This, of course, does not mean everything happens in public.

Chief and I agree not to include any of the newer, on-the-radar spaces or events in this document. These spots are friendly and social. I would not go unnoticed. Given my recent personal boundary issues, we do not think I am ready for that kind of engagement.

I whittle my assignment down to three locations. At each, I am stimulated, welcomed, and left alone. The locations:

1. MBad African Bead Museum
2. Detroit Institute of Arts
3. Youngworld

MBad African Bead Museum

Several acres of grassy land, buildings (covered with splintered mirrors, bright paint, bead murals), and a full-bodied series of installations make up this indoor/outdoor space that explores ways Africa informs and intertwines with American experience. Even though freeways are on one side and a busy city street lines the other, it is a calm, sweet spot to be.

Looking at, or trying to look into, mirror shards gives a disconcerting reflection. You see yourself and what is behind you in fragments. The experience makes clear what we might intellectually know but forget emotionally: you never view your image in a mirror, just some sphere of self-awareness or lack of.

The installation "Iron Teaching Rocks How to Rust" tells of imposed loss, decay, and corrosion on people wrenched from their homes, traditions, and cultures. One scene depicts a deserted dinner table covered with plates, bowls, knives, spoons, and forks, all made of iron. A few years ago, you and I, Hoss, on a case in Senegal, learned to eat with our hands. The sequence of fingers to food to mouth prepares saliva and digestion for a happy eating experience. Here, enforced use of cutlery disrupts the potential harmony. Eaters consume but are hampered.

A tall stack of plates in the table's center makes me think of Charles Dickens's character Miss Havisham, the bitter bride, left at the altar, choosing to live inside her white gown and ruined mansion, leaving her table strewn with wedding breakfast and cake as she sinks into misery, perhaps self-chastisement.

The comparison illustrates two forms of punishment. One comes from outside, and the other is self-imposed. The diners are forced to comply with new rules. In contrast, my position parallels Miss Havisham's. She chose her dissolution. And, well, I fucked up by blurring boundaries with a handsome enemy. My dis-ease generated by myself is reversible. I have the luxury to make amends and wrest back some professional and personal control. Not as easy an option for the kidnapped eaters at the rusted table.

The museum itself is inside a house, holding bins of beautiful, handmade, variously-sized and marked ceremonial beads referred to in the literature as "textbooks packed with information." Their meanings are impenetrable, but I feel their pull and an urge to engage with their clues, force, data.

I come here mornings to pray. Am reminded that I am not an individual but a soul in a series of souls. Some keep watch over me, and others are out to harm me. I pay attention to both.

My specific professional skill is to identify, track down, and hold accountable the high-level criminals who think of themselves as too big to bust. I am capable of but am uninterested in punishing low- and mid-level offenders. Enough of them get apprehended. It is unfair and does not solve our crime problem. (I do, however, use the low-level offenders to lead me to their bosses.) My Italian laceless oxfords hold a special place in my heart because I got them after one of our greatest takedowns: a Count, representing old European aristocracy, apparently untouchable, who was involved with international human trafficking.

I soon get information on a drug ring with a Detroit presence. Its leaders are not based here. But I will cool it. (Okay, Chief Hoss.) I will not make a bust but possibly lay solid groundwork for one elsewhere.

I get on the radar of a mid-level worker in the ring by posing as an agent for an unidentified organization.

Getting them to follow me requires specific strategy. When you want to be tracked, you must make the potential tracker believe it is their idea to track you. As long as they believe they are the ones in charge, you are okay.

Detroit Institute of Arts

We have an agency DIA membership. I visit whenever I come to town. Here are a few favorites.

Great Hall—Armor

In the Great Hall, just up the steps from the museum entrance, there are several suits of full metal armor in glass cases. My early education requires dressing, training, and fighting in plate armor. It takes tremendous energy to get the suits on and off—not to mention to become accustomed to what it is like, because of their heft and weight distribution, to wear them in battle. The goal of this type of combat: stab opponents through the helmet's slim horizontal slit and deliver a lethal pierce to the eye region. It is a challenging, specialized form of combat that takes me back to my early roots.

Detroit Industry Murals, Diego Rivera

These twenty-seven panels depicting industry at Ford Motor Company remind me why I chose what I do. Yes, the murals are magnificent and transmit a tribute to workers, doctors, manufacturers, and scientists in the 1930s. They convey what great things can happen given the time, money, and space. Looking at them, I cannot ignore corporate captains of industry. Large-scale art projects are often financed by these people. They are just the types of criminals I excel at catching. High-Level Businessmen. I am not saying Edsel Ford or William Valentiner (responsible, I believe, for commissioning the work) were or were not criminal. But they might well have been. And anyway they lived and dwelled in the kinds of powerful circles with those who certainly were.

I consistently keep *these kind* on my radar.

Following my Chief's orders to re-group and contemplate, I also spend time with art that is less directly connected to my profession. I wander around and find so many pieces I love. I will describe two paintings.

Martha and Mary Magdalene, Caravaggio

A painting of the supposed moment Martha persuades her sister Mary to become Christian. Both sisters wear green and red. Martha's clothes are shabby, and Mary's are elegant. Martha, bent low in the lower left corner, implores Mary, towering on the right like a radiant sun or holy beam, to convert. Mary's transition is portrayed with a lush, heartfelt, relieved kind of facial expression that I am not sure exists in real life. But I hope it does. Her body suggests an engorgement I associate with pregnancy, but it surely comes from being infused with things otherworldly. Caravaggio makes a convincing case. She has a rich inner life plus a special heart (huge, forgiving, wide open), which may explain what so deeply touched Jesus.

L'Amour (For Panic D.J.), Elizabeth Murray

This blue and red painting/sculpture (it pulls away from the wall, so you can also see its wooden back) is a committed tribute to the power and potential of theatricality off the stage.

Its eye space in the lower center and top that stretches up vertically like a piled up hairdo or tall hat makes me think of a complex, carefully crafted mask or persona. It holds the shape of three question marks, and the center image is a table with broken legs, suggesting torn arteries and damaged vessels, twisting and turning away from the middle.

I happen to have briefly met the artist, Murray, a native English speaker, and her husband, Bob Holman, a magnetic performance poet, years ago when we investigate their building. We learn Holman performs under a moniker, Panic D.J., and wears a question mark on his lapel.

If this painting was titled *Love (For Bob)*, I would say it illustrates the heartache, histrionics, romance, tedium, and aches within a marital structure. But every element of the painting refers to things masquerade. For example, the title's foreign language and use of Holman's stage name. Its shape as his performance prop is dramatic.

Murray champions, or at least makes the case, to intentionally weave these elements into a traditional, potentially routine, dull, and accepted convention like marriage. *Hold on,* she seems to say, *This is convention, but we can still make it riotous, edgy, iffy, and erotic.*

I visit the DIA mid day, a time I routinely feel overwhelmed by gruesome realities encountered in my line of work. I take time to look at beautiful, carefully considered things people construct, even if they do not always behave that way.

Is it so hard to understand how I blur emotional boundaries with the criminal? (He was very handsome.) Even a carefully trained agent like me is not immune to the perils of isolation. I believe in but perhaps am not cut out for intimacy.

Maybe what generates my trouble is not allowing for or ignoring personal needs.

Isn't that why people are drawn to what happens in Detroit? The emphasis on goodwill and community? The more I ride my bike around this city, the lonelier I feel. I see people holding art critiques, gathering at barbeques, bazaars, dance labs, community garden sessions, cultural exchange projects. I see increasingly cohesive neighborhoods. They have something that I, in my position, do not.

I continue making progress in attracting my tail.

Youngworld

In Emily Bronte's novel *Wuthering Heights,* Cathy—completely sincere, possibly deranged—says, "I am Healthcliff."

I, coming from similar places, say, "I *am* Youngworld."

We both deeply consider, and engage with, the value, and limits, of covert operations.

The building is behind a chain link fence, on an overgrown lot, just off a strip of Mt. Elliott, a place once packed with businesses. Now a few still thrive, while others are waning or gone.

It is off the beaten track, in Detroit but near the edge of Hamtramck, which is a hub of the kinds of activity I, as earlier explained, must painfully avoid.

Nothing about YW says "art" unless you happen to catch the once-a-month openings.

I brave three and go unnoticed. The inside is vast and has poor lighting. I figure out how to enter the rest of the time and illuminate the darkness with my flashlight and plug into whatever technology is needed. This is my go-to place to spend time alone, absorb exhibitions' oblique charisma, consider how and why they at once throw off and ignite and the ways they reaffirm my dedication to espionage.

No surprise, then, that it turns out to be the perfect place to lure and eventually confront the mid-level drug worker I get to trail me. But I don't want to get ahead of my story.

a. Jeremy Couillard, *Believes in Reincarnation Hates Hugs*

Two words: Stimulation, Insistence.

We at the agency spend time thinking of and preparing for a post-collapse future: the darkness, the end points, and all that will be no longer. Therefore, focus on needs: light, temperature, tools, protection. Purified water, preserved food.

In contrast, Couillard's acid bright animations blow past that. They portray a *future* future or what occupies *post* post-collapse. That includes morphed, functioning beings bumping close enough to—not against or into—one another to generate erotic currency. It is hot, intimate, watching these organisms dwelling in a toxic and questionably sustainable mess. Their life quality and lifespan are up in the air, but one thing is solidly constant in this world: pleasure, various forms, non-idealized, unrelated to reproduction.

See, this is the kind of solving strategy that parallels my job. Start with a case or problem and then refigure, reimagine, and manipulate what can be done.

Lastly, back to his title, when dwelling in the unthinkable, why hug when you can get it on?

b. Claire Ashley, *Lank Limp Lemons Suck*

You can spend enjoyable time with this title. Say it out loud, in different orders: lank, lemon, limp, suck. Toy with various meanings and oppositions as entry points to permutations of this show.

Ashley makes paintings, not on rack, but on polymer sheeting. She pumps the material up and forms airy, bouncy cushions you want to jump on or collapse into, but be careful because they are unreliable. They are too big or small—in constant motion, inflating, deflating, possibly toxic—so you cannot really do either.

The paintings respectfully and buoyantly take over, grow into, and perhaps dig into the gallery's floor and walls like bulbs, roots, or limbs. At the same time, they suggest an astral conspiracy. Are they about to take off? Or get sucked up? And one more thing: they exude the potential to come to life like a doll or stuffed animal. Hopefully the transition is into friendly and not wicked forms.

By respectful I mean they work and coexist with YW's space in ways that remind me of the marriage between our friends Hanch and Jennifer. When the two first meet, Jennifer is a robot, but she (through Hanch's love) develops true human feelings and organs (digestive and sexual).

Ashley's works suggest a similar potential to transform unexpectedly; they *are* but also *in a process of being.*

c. Lan Tuazon, *Bad Grass Never Dies*

The exhibition—and its title's lovely sequence of hard consonants—helps me understand the full complexity of the word cycle.

And it helps me understand ways we mythologize concepts like beginning and end.

It utilizes indoor and outdoor space.

Inside (among other things) recyclable waste vessels (plastic bottles, containers and cones) are sliced in pristine halves, meticulously ordered and arranged. YW now looks like a petri dish.

Inside I feel a pull downward.

In part because titles with words like "cradle," "grave," "pit," and "peak" turn things around and inside out.

I want to focus on the burial ritual performed on opening night because it plays a solid role in concluding my time in Detroit.

Full disclosure: I have personal issues with burial since reading Edger Allan Poe as a child. As an adult, I work through this with self burials (time limited) and yogic breathing, which helps but does not solve the problem.

Tuazon digs a Pit of Mundus (hole of the world) in front of the gallery and leaves it empty and gaping during the opening until the evening's end, when she calls guests to assemble around it. She asks that we sacrifice (toss into the pit) items that no longer serve us. She starts with her own contribution. Even from my position, I panic. Even as I understand, my panic misses her point. The fact she suggests they transition and wind up in dirt and pass downward, possibly to a better underworld place, does nothing to lessen my dis-ease.

I get a brief, potent fever when she says, "Take a deep breath. These things no longer occupy the same air as you."

Something cracks. In a good way. "No longer occupy the same air as you" does not mean writhing in agony (my image), nostrils and throat plugged up with dirt.

My comprehension *was* hampered by my over valuing oxygen. Not every*thing* needs breath, and once you take breath out of the equation, there is nothing frightening about burial. Oxygen dependence as construction. Tuazon shepherds me to an understanding: transitioning from oxygen dependence to oxygen independence is not necessarily horrifying.

I leave after witnessing guests get rid of whatever, and her seal the hole with things plastic. I feel light, mobile, reshuffled.

I choose this spot to meet my mid-level drug tracker. Regularity is key to drawing attention, so over the next week, I return to again at the same time each evening. When the light is waning but is not dark and I stand on the now dirt-covered pit, I think of the sacrificed objects, nestling in their new home, perhaps travelling downward, oxygen-free. I notice him (tall, stooped) behind me, increasingly close, several times. When he is finally close enough, I turn, spin, kick him to the ground, and put my foot on his neck.

We converse.

I get needed information, help him up, and massage his neck to undo any damage my assault caused before I send him home.

My head clears. My heart opens.

Chief Hoss, here is your journalistic art document. Hopefully it meets your criteria. Please consider letting me back in. I am not being critical. This assignment was probably helpful, but I prefer solving crime.

Respectfully,
Agent Paula Regossy

5 Dose

Paula

Recuperating in Detroit I roam at night. Repeatedly return to a particular house and sense this story, Eva's story.

Sometimes, late at night, I walk neighborhood streets and stand in front of homes and sense stories. I do not make them up. Sensing is not the same as inventing.

Now I stand in front of a house and sense Eva. She was born here and still periodically lives here. Or, more accurately, on, in, and around its roof, eaves, gutters, grass, and trees. The house is in a town that is small enough so you can still see stars and sky and get to know people. From the porch, you might smell onions, lilacs, coffee, soap, and pastries that are baking. You might smell smoke from fireplaces, cigarettes, and cigars.

Eva grew up wearing blouses and skirts to school. (Thin cotton in warm weather, felt or wool in cold.)

Her parents owned a hair salon that also offered massage and beauty treatments.

Eva and her mother, Laura, looked alike. They were both on the short side and had hazel eyes, full lips, and curly dark hair. Her father was tall, blond, and blue-eyed.

After school, Eva visited her parents' business to assist with the health, hair, and beauty treatments. She wore an apron over her clothes when doing this.

Every day, not long before the salon closed at six, a woman walked by. She never came inside but regularly waved to Eva, who waved back. The woman wore elegant clothes, like satin dresses (gray, maroon, indigo) and ankle boots. In winter, she covered them with a brocade coat. She always wore hats, usually with some kind of feathers or fur attached.

One warm fall day, she motioned for Eva to step outside. She smiled at her and leaned down with a palm open. In her hand, nestled within a silver muffin cup, sat a small petit four that had white icing and a pink rose on top.

"I watch you, Eva," she said. "I know and have a good sense of who you are and what you need."

Eva stood silent.

"Eat this. It is a dose that will give you a life different from everyone else. Life is wonderful, but this dose gives you choices. You will be happier in the long run because you will learn to see things from different perspectives."

Eva took the petit four and ate it with the smallest bites she could manage. It was the best thing she had ever eaten. She savored each taste as long as she could before swallowing.

She returned inside. Her mother, Laura, asked, "What is on your lips?"

"Powder from the sweet that fancy lady gave me."

"Who?"

"That lady who walks by every day with the pretty clothes and hats."

"What an imagination you have, my dear. It runs, runs, runs. An Olympic champion!"

That night in bed, Eva opened her eyes from a deep sleep. She felt restless, excited. She looked at the moon shining outside her window, moved toward it. What was this? Changes. Big Changes. She had fur, four legs, paws, and could leap. She was a squirrel. A flying squirrel. Her new body knew what to do. She leaped out the window and landed gently on the branch of a tree. From it, she looked at her bed and saw her human self lying there.

"The dose! I am in bed and outside at once," she said.

In bed as a girl, outside as a squirrel.

For the first two nights, she played outside alone because other squirrels slept at that time. But the third night she met one other squirrel. His name was Buff. She understood he had been given a dose, too. They sensed but never discussed that they each had human lives in the day and special squirrel time at night.

Eva and Buff spent all night running, jumping, flying, gathering food, and making out. For years to come, they lived as squirrels, but so many things about them were not true for squirrels. Their life span was long, and they survived hits by cars. They mated—and not just twice yearly to breed—but nightly for stimulation and to express love.

Human Eva grew, graduated from high school, and went to college. She met, fell in love with, and married a man named Tom, who was from a rich Canadian farm family. Eva, now fully adult, is recognizable as the Eva then (dark eyes, wide cheeks, space between her two front teeth), but she dresses differently. Last time I saw her, she wore a giant funnel-neck top and a pencil skirt. The time before that it was the same skirt with a snug-fitting v-neck top under a cape that swept down her back. In warm weather, she wears sleeveless shift dresses with scarves and necklaces. Her shoes, boots, and sandals all have round toes and sturdy heels.

Each day, Eva functions as a human. For the most part, happily. She loves Tom. She really does. As a woman. No matter where she and Tom live and travel, she always finds herself at home, as a squirrel, at night. She never misses a day with Tom or a night with Buff. There are moments when her squirrel life bleeds into her human one. For example, when she wants to store nuts in her mouth or bite into an unshelled one. Or when she stops on the sidewalk, squats, and peers into cement cracks to picture the complex life nestled into the soil below.

Every few years Tom asks, "What about children?"

She does not answer.

It is a happy life.

Years and years go by.

Her father dies.

She and her mother close the salon.

Tom dies. Eva is late-middle-aged by this time.

They never had children. She never thought she would lose her husband before her mother. Her heart is broken, but she still has Buff.

Laura gets sick.

Eva hires home help but visits her mother daily.

She is so sad to see the decline. At one medical visit the doctor says, "You need to be around people, Laura dear."

This jars Laura because she knows it is best for her not to be around people. Why? Because she knows they do not want to be around her. She hears what they think: *Oh, Laura. Look at you now.*

Soiling your underpants, drooling. And you smell. You used to be so elegant, so funny. What a good cook you once were.

She hears this as clearly as if it came out of their mouths and wonders, *Why would I want to be around these people?*

They are good, healthy people.

What good would it do to repel them? What good would it do to subject them to my discharges, moans, and pain? My sadness? Let them enjoy what time they have left. They will get where I am soon enough.

But she says none of this, only stares at the doctor with her eyes, which are still hazel but now dull and no longer keen.

Then, later, at home, she asks Eva, "Why can't I be alone and drift out to sea? Or soar up to the sky into pillowy clouds? Or fly over the desert or drill down to inner earth?"

Eva feels a jolt. This is the longest and most coherent series of thoughts her mother has put together in years. She sits close and strokes her hand.

Laura is silent for the next two days.

The third day, Eva leaves Laura at home with the caretaker and walks to the store for milk. She sees the woman with the fancy clothes on the street.

It has been years, yet she looks the same. She approaches Eva and hands her a tiny box.

"Please, give this to your mother," she says.

Eva takes the box, opens it. Nestled inside sits a petit four, cream colored and dark brown.

"It will give your beautiful mother peace and joy."

Eva realizes she is lucky to live half of her life as a sort of flying squirrel. She trusts this woman completely. That night, she sits on a branch with Buff. They sit close together, look up to the sky, and sense spirits and stars, all separate yet together. She thinks of her dear mother: that elegant hair, the tightly rolled cabbage leaves, the crusty baked bread. Her back bent from leaning over customers' bodies, her fingers raw from bleach.

The next morning, Eva puts the petit four on a porcelain plate. "Mom, good morning. I brought you breakfast!"

Her mother recognizes her only sometimes now, but her eyes widen at the fancy sweet on the elegant plate. She places it between her thumb and index finger, brings it to her mouth, takes a few delicate bites. This is how she used to eat. Lately, she's been grabbing food and smashing it into her mouth. But not this morning. When she is finished, she gives her daughter a smile. Radiant, toothy, and wide. She holds Eva's hand, lies back, looks out of the window. After a while, she sighs. Her eyes close. Her skin is luminous. Eva holds her hand and feels it grow cool then cold. She sits there for hours. Later in the afternoon, she hears chirping. Outside on the tree branch is a black bird staring at her. Its eyes are hazel, the same green-and-brown blend of her mother's. She knows there, now, lives her mother. She waves, and the bird nods. She cannot wait to go to sleep and wake up as a squirrel. When she does later that night, she leaps from her room to the branch. Her mother, the bird, is perched there. Buff joins them. They all put their heads together and gently rub.

Now, when the stars are bright enough or there is a full moon, I see the three of them romping at night. Sometimes on the roof, sometimes on branches, sometimes soaring through the sky together.

6 Staredown

Agent Joan

I grew up with a big extended family in a small crowded space. For the most part, we got along. There were occasional arguments, a few fights. Some of those ended with a hug, a smile, or a scowl. Others ended in threats or physical violence. None were terrible or irreversible until my older brother, Tad, got in a nasty confrontation with his childhood friend Mick and died. But that incident did not take place within our family or inside our home.

Tad is the one person I love. He got hot-headed-ly into a duel with his childhood buddy over Sara, a girl, a fine girl. My brother lost the match, which was really just a bet, and lost his life.

That death taught me this: there are no winners in a duel.

After the match Mick, the supposed victor, had what his parents called a breakdown. He moved east, renounced things worldly, spent his time fasting, meditating, and helping the poor. Sara, the girl, abandoned by both suitors, also had a supposed breakdown. She stopped talking to humans, but collected various pets and, eventually, opened an animal shelter.

When Tad was challenged to the duel or suggested the match himself (I do not know the exact truth of the story), he did not opt to consider other possible ways to address the situation or his feelings. For example: try another course of action or share Sara with Mick or give her up or just try to love Mick or decide to love both at once.

Or resolve things with a respectful stare down.

Instead, he chose the old fashioned, sure-to-end-badly route: death match.

My family was sad but not devastated by Tad's death. They are a big extended group. They are also nomadic. With so many siblings, aunts, uncles, cousins, and offspring coming and going, no one concentrates fully or for long on a single loss—even if it is of someone as special as Tad.

I say *my family*, but I do not now think of them that way. I used to. I used to think of us—*my family* and me—as we, but since Tad's death, I think of them as *that family*. Separate from me.

I, perhaps selfishly, believe I lost the most from that duel. Tad, wherever he is since losing, thrives. Afterlife is special. This I know. Mick and Sara might retain scars, but they both find useful, generous ways to navigate life after the tragedy. Not me. Until I meet Paula, Tad's death damaged me. Time stopped. Stopped but did not stand still. Time got deformed, mean, squashed down.

I imagine someone hearing this story say that Tad's death did not cause my damage, that I was damaged before. I understand the point. A non-damaged person can go through tragic events and, even with wounds, function. A non-damaged person can face tragedy, have difficulty healing, but still move on. For an event to cause time stoppage or cramping, damage had to be there, lurking to begin with. I cannot argue with this.

Instead, let me try to explain what I encountered after the match.

For a while, I stopped growing. Then I shrunk.

People no longer saw me as me but as a vegetal blur. Like a dandelion seed head or dust ball.

Another thing happened: my new body stopped respecting gravity. I was permanently airborne, hovering or flying. And I emitted a sound, a buzz.

"Stop buzzing. It makes me nervous," said my dad. "Buzzing means insects. When I think insect, I think swat. But you are my daughter, my love. I do not want to swat you. But what if I cannot tell the difference? What if one day I hear buzz and think BUG and smash you?"

At this point I learned to control my buzz volume and to keep myself high up in the air—or at a wide horizontal distance—out of any person's reach. Something else happened. My senses sharpened. I saw and heard from a distance as well as close up. This put a new spin on my world and on my re-tooled position within it. Paula, an old colleague of mom's, learned about me and my condition and visited. Rather than lament my condition she saw it as great potential. Her faith and direction opened the door for a new, meaningful life and career as an undercover operative who could sense, and transmit, highly sensitive data.

7 Difference not Value

Agent Jos

When I write my name for the first time, our teacher claps and encourages the class to clap. I feel an initial glow but self-check.

Through our school window I see the sun, animals, and vegetation. I understand these trees, squirrels, and birds are occupied with their own feats. It is fall, time for seasonal adjustments. Birds head south, squirrels prepare for hibernation, leaves turn red, orange, yellow and drop to the ground.

I consider: does each bird, squirrel, leaf, tree have an individual name, and a version of writing it? No.

Can I fly, sleep through winter, turn colors, and drop twenty feet gently? No.

None of us has *every*thing. Each of us, *some*thing. Wildlife and vegetation are at least as important as I am. *I* have and can write a name. *They* are wired to seasonally adjust. The contrasts illustrate our difference, not value.

Writing my name brings a taste of mastery and the headiness that comes with it. But I sense the high is flimsy. It's a lift like getting good track speeds, making clever science models, or hitting tough notes in choir.

So I tell myself, *Be suspicious*. Like with handsome vampires and other things hard to resist but perilous.

The specific skill elevates my pupil position, gives me power. And, like someone in the Spiderman series says, "With power comes responsibility."

But I need help navigating that.

Over the next few years, I turn my lens inward, hoping to discover other skills.

I learn they are not:
- Track, science models, choir
- Music, math, drawing
- Planting flowers
- Knitting, swimming, embroidery

I learn they are:
- Observation
- Research
- Recordkeeping

Why? Because I spot and document various forms of trouble (scuffles, thefts, pranks) no one else even notices and track their occurrence in consistent pockets of time: before and after school, during recess and mandatory class meditation, when our teacher Steve dips into deep psychic space or maybe sleeps.

I accumulate information (who, what, when) but have no idea what to do with it. No one to share it with. I am alone and poorly equipped. In other words, lost.

Then Steve shares these lines from poet W.H. Auden:

I and the public know
What all school children learn,
Those to whom evil is done
Do evil in return

And, for the first time, I sense the complexity of crime—the twisted tapestry of victims, perpetrators and the boundaries, often blurred, between them. I am fascinated, illuminated, but have no strategy for action. To do more I need to know more. But how?

Each morning Steve starts lessons saying, "Be Here Now."

I never thought about what that meant. Just like I never thought about the colorful, detailed butterfly drawings behind his desk or his Greenpeace t-shirts.

But one morning, when he says, "Be Here Now," I get an idea: make a list (nonjudgmental) separating my *cannots* from cans.

At this point I cannot:
– Solve or stop wrongdoings

At this point I can:
– Cultivate surveillance skills
– Be more detailed when recording and filing data
– Participate in group meditation rather than use the time to spy

I enjoy the focus my new skills and meditation provide and learn an important lesson: limitations can structure rather than squash a rise to power.

Yet this newfound growth unearths a gap in Spiderman's "With great power comes great responsibility" construct. Where is happiness?

Name writing brings advantages but not joy. Surveillance and documentation, in contrast, elate me. I wish I could ask him his thoughts about this. Specifically, does he see a place for happiness with power and himself? I cannot. So, alone, consider that maybe he is not as brave as I thought because he does not address joy. Joy is emotionally risky. It requires courage. You have to give something personal to get it, and if you fail, you fall into a bad place. Maybe one you never are able to leave.

But I am not sure. I just would like to talk with Spiderman about it. Would like to hear his thoughts about my thoughts. I am not someone who rushes to judgment.

While I push those questions away, I face the fact that I dislike the word "happy" and other terms—"glad," "joy," "delight"—that supposedly define it. Happy is something I viscerally sense, but words are a pale match for my sensation.

Then, during a volunteer lunch shift in the teachers' lounge where I wash cups, wipe down the sink, and expand my surveillance from school students to staff, I have a breakthrough. Listening, as usual, to teachers discuss eastern philosophy, work commutes, rock bands, and back pain, I hear Steve say he is launching a weekly Vladimir Nabokov reading group. He opens this first session by quoting the great author's line "Little sob in the spine."

My life changes.

"Little sob in the spine." These words nail happy. Or nail what happy means to me.

"Little sob in the spine." That is how I feel listening to opera and eating fall apples with grandma. It is how I feel during my surveillance sessions. It is how I want to feel always. Even if I sense this is unrealistic.

After Steve quotes the line, he turns things over to our student teacher, Paula, who gives a short analysis on why the phrase works so beautifully.

"'Little sob in the spine is successful,'" she says, "first, because of the alliteration. 'Cry in the back,' for example, would not work."

Second, because of a series of opposing forces.

a) Pairing an emotion with a nerve/bone system rather than a soft organ.

Consider: Sob in the throat/Sob in the gut/Sob in the heart. See? All less effective.

Other examples of contrast:
b) Sob (uncontrolled) vs spine (regulator)
c) Sob (moist) vs spine (solid)
d) And, little sob, shows big size does not matter.

Convulsion in the spine would not work. Or tidal wave. Or hurricane.

Little sob joins other potent mini thrills: pinprick, dewdrop, eyelash flutter against any body part.

That was my first introduction to Paula, who became my lifelong mentor. I would be nowhere without her.

"Little sob in the spine." Those words enchant me, send sensations up and down my legs, arms, back, stomach, chest, and neck.

Now that I have words to express *happy* I narrow down where to find mine. Surveillance with a purpose.

Meaning I hope to do something I enjoy for the larger good.

Over the next few months, I see Paula around our neighborhood (skate park, library, community garden), usually wearing her trademark shirtdress and laceless oxfords. It is early fall. One day, grandma and I run into her in the grocery store. The two make an immediate connection, talking about opera, medical marijuana, and almond based pastries. I am so surprised, in a good way, by this back and forth that I neglect my usual grocery store beat. (I spend regular, careful surveillance time in this large market, scoping out the shoppers, cashiers, butchers, and the produce managers along with building elements: window seals, door gaskets, bathroom stalls, faucets, and soap dispensers. Even then I understand people-watching takes you only so far. You must also attend to "innocuous" structures of dailiness.)

After seeing Paula connect with grandma, I am comfortable sharing my Spiderman concerns. I tell her I respect him. I wish I could ask him about power, responsibility, and if there is room in his quote for happiness. I am so curious about what he would have to say. She tells me my question is a good one but might be too much for him. She suggests I restrict myself to keywords in his original formulation: "power," "responsibility."

I could take away something like this:

If you have power, it is your responsibility to acknowledge it.

But because the original quote does not include the word "happy," I should not look for things linked to happiness there. Spiderman is mission driven. He is probably not the person I should ask about happy. But, I can find answers to my happiness question elsewhere. She reminds me how much help I got from Vladimir Nabokov. Maybe I should accept what I got from Spiderman and now turn to others for answers to my happiness questions.

Over time Paula teaches me that my area of interest is a bona fide profession: criminal arts. It involves detecting, tracking, solving, tracing, protecting, busting, compiling, reporting, healing, rehabilitating, and punishing those involved. She and her agency chief, Hoss, will take me through rigorous training, and I will have a lifelong espionage career that might bring, at least intermittent, "little sob in the spine."

This Nabokov word lesson is the first in a long series that become indispensable and contribute to my success in the field.

Paula teaches me the importance of relying on a source—or sources. Sometimes you rely on just one, completely, faithfully, monogamously, and follow those orders to a T. Other times you work with a variety and need to weigh and balance who and what to attend to. In this case, before making a final decision, I spread out ingredients (clues, facts, ideas), close my eyes, and consider. In each case, information is everywhere. You just have to know when, where, and how to track it down.

8 Same Sky

Agent Nadea

"The Brain—is wider than the Sky," wrote Emily Dickinson. It is a beautiful line. But problematic. First, some brains are cramped, narrow. They have *potential to be* wider than the sky. Second, a brain by itself is limited. A brain, together with a heart, under good guidance, holds infinite potential.

If I could sit down with Dickinson, I might suggest, "The Brain and Heart, trained and directed, can be wider than the Sky." Not a pretty line at all but one that covers more bases.

I, a detective, not poet, sit in mom's sewing room. I have just left her, dad, both sets of grandparents, and my little sister, Rose. I am the only "living" (earthbound) member of the group.

Multi-sphere communication is something we do, have always done. I am not here to defend or convince you of its existence or link to spirituality, only to say it is a consistent family practice that widens our brains and hearts. Ben, my brother, who lives way up in the northern part of our state, communicates this way and so do our cousins. When we visit, we do it together.

Mom loved this sewing room, even slept here at the end of her life. It holds stacks of books and unused journals. (I write in one now.) It holds embroidered tablecloths and napkins, stacked neatly in the linen cupboard dad built. Dresses hang in the closet. Today I wear her white muslin caftan with bees (jet black, bright yellow) embroidered along the neck and sleeve lines. Mom loved bees and their robust presence in our city. She was proud that certain buildings in and around our business district used hives in their architectural ornamentation. Maybe because of her I imagine honey bees hunkering down, making food, feeding offspring.

This is my story of their lives—comforting but perhaps factually flawed.

It is a cool spring day. I bring this journal out to our porch and write as I take in blossoming trees, kids jumping rope, fresh air.

It is late afternoon. Communing with family is a needed break from my job as a criminal agent, a profession I am devoted to. When I say devoted, I mean obsessed—but that is a harsh word, and I don't want you to stop reading. Or listening.

My job.

Without it I am nothing.

Paula, my superior, provides specific brain/heart training and support essential for criminal agent effectiveness. Without that, we agents are nothing. With it, we can be wider than the sky.

On a human scale.

So *wider than the sky*, relatively speaking.

My crime-fighting career stems from personal tragedy. Our beautiful Rose was murdered as a teenager. Throat slit. Otherwise physically unharmed.

This note was left on her body:

You're a Beauty
But
You are not the one

A nasty construction.

I sensed, even back then and pre-trained, that there would be other victims. There were.

Rose.

I always told her, "If I die before you, never worry because my ghost will settle in your body so we can always be together."

This was our game, our joke, and hilarious because an early death for either of us was inconceivable.

Multi-sphere communication is not goal driven. It is not for asking Emily Dickinson about brains and hearts, for asking mom how she learned stumpwork embroidery or Rose about her murder.

We use the process to pass time together in the same way other timeouts are soothing—like sitting together on a porch or hill or beach or living room couch. Times we merge, rather than volley. Then, restored, go our separate ways.

Hanch, dad's client and close family friend, visits from Denmark just after Rose is murdered.

"Cry," he says to Ben and me. "You have to take this time now and let yourselves grieve for your sister. Otherwise it will be so much harder to move forward. Cry. Cry together. Cry alone. Cry in the morning, cry at night. Cry when you play the piano, cry when you jump rope. Listen to these operas." He hands us a small stack of LP's. "Especially *Madame Butterfly*, a sadistic story with beautiful music. The cruelty and loveliness together will make you wail."

He hands us a book. "Fairytales. Truly devastating, most of them. If you read 'Hansel and Gretel,' 'Little Red Riding Hood,' 'The Little Mermaid,' you will sob. Some versions have revisions with happy endings, but you can always find the original, brutal ones. Even with the revisions, just think of what those poor children had to endure. The man who wrote 'The Little Mermaid,' Hans Christian Anderson, is from my country. He said mermaids are the saddest creatures because they don't have tears and therefore suffer more. I agree with him. But you two are human and have tears. Use them to lessen your suffering."

During the next few weeks, Ben and I listen to opera, read fairytales, grieve. We hurt. We act and zone out.

I cannot revisit that post-murder period in any more personal detail.

Hanch spends more time with our parents than my brother and I do. The three hunker down in dad's wood workshop. One afternoon I bring them a tray of tea and hear Hanch ask, "How can it be that we and that killer share the same sky?"

This is my first experience with the value of a solid clue.

The same sky.

Yes, I think. *How can we share it?* But we do.

I feel a stir of excitement. The world is wide-ranging and apparently random. But we all share a sky. That structure offers, absolutely, the possibility of me tracking down and apprehending Rose's murderer.

And, after Hanch introduces me to Paula, with her guidance and instruction, I do.

But that is a much longer story I will share with you another time.

9 Lines of Duty

Agent Elizabeth

I was having a tough time when a friend said, "Love makes your soul crawl out from its hiding place."

This helped immensely but not at first because I understood her to mean love as passionate, permanent partnership and thought, *Right*. That interpretation reflected my limitations, not her meaning. The more I thought, the more I considered her love suggested various and possibly magical forms of affection for people, places, moments and things in and across the universe. Each of us must track down and cultivate loves that work for us personally.

If we want them.

I believe we do.

"Love makes your soul crawl out from its hiding place." The line comes from Zora Neale Hurston, who dwells somewhere in the multi-sphere. We never met in person. I call her "friend" not to mislead you but because friend is the best definition of what we mean to each other. Her words are always there for me, and I, in turn, am always there for them. Thank you, Zora. Thank you, words. Thank you, friend.

Great loves that move my soul out from its (sometimes bleak, sometimes comforting) cupboard are specific cities, spaces, bodies and, most of all, my job, which is tracking and busting crime.

I am a detective, partly because of personal history and constitution and partly because of what and who come along.

My trigger story: early teens, evening, chasing Boots, our dog, I stumble across a dead body, somehow get home (that part remains a blur), and my parents contact authorities. Dad, an officer, understands and helps with follow-up procedure, including my having to go to the station and detail what I was doing and saw. The victim is our neighbor. Her name is June.

My life is divided by pre- and post- that murder. Post introduces me to Paula and my calling, which is detective work. But there are horrible conditions before that, and those play equal parts in this journey, starting with a series of bad emotional homes. Suspended, spiky spaces with nowhere to land. Clammy baths to sink unpleasantly into. Shrill, blaring sounds that are insistent, impossible to shut out. Each condition feels right, deserved. Each allows me to maintain my devotion to June. Each lets me say, "Neighbor, I won't abandon you. Ever."

For short periods, I look at the sky, stroke Boots, and watch Zeb, June's widower, tend to his bees. All with minimal engagement. Personal momentum for me equals shirking responsibility to her. Staying stagnant, dis-eased, keeps my aim true, our allegiance solid.

There are moments when I feel a pang, as if there could be more, but I shove them away. These moments happen when Boots puts her head on my lap, when I hear music and when I see Zeb trudge to his hives, shoulders hunched over, head hanging.

My parents take me to a health professional who diagnoses trauma and suggests giving me time, space, and support rather than push for a cure.

The murder. I recount the scene to my parents, the police, the professional, and will do so now for you. Early evening, chasing Boots, I find our neighbor, June, in her backyard, lying flat. Mouth and ears stuffed with soil. There is a note, typed and pinned to her blouse that reads, *You don't really care for music, do you?* It is a gold pin, vintage, substantial and decorative. It's the kind used to close a skirt or sweater.

The scene hits me with various horrible sensations but mostly with a desperate sliver of hope that something is wrong with me, not her. So wrong that I mis-see, mis-take, make-up what I witness. Being right, something I usually take pride in, is not, now, what I want. I want to be wrong. But I am not. When I recall the scene, any of it, the worst part is always the note. Because those words prove June is not dead from a burst of bad weather, a rabid beast, or an angry spirit—but because of a human being who performed with intention.

I make decisions to:

Find who did this and strategically retaliate.

So shift slowly from damp dependence toward a new, heat inducing state: anger.

Warmth generates modest movement. I leave my bleak homes for fleeting, frantic moments. But why?

To flatten under failure?

At least, before, I had a mission—or believed I did.

Now I'm useless. And mean. I hate these new spaces and myself. I ignore my parents, our piano, Zeb, his bees. I grit my teeth at the kids walking to school, biking, jumping rope, and playing organized sports. Scratch myself, force-barf, shave my head un-strategically. That period was just as immersive as the bad homes but seems reckless, unproductive. At least before my loyalties were clear, my mind-set purposeful.

But ire expends energy. I need sleep and finally can. Bed sheets that felt clammy are now warm, dry. Boots sleeps in my arms rather than under the bed or across the room.

Sleep brings momentum. I step outside, stroke vegetation. I sit in mom's tree house, survey delivery trucks and kids hanging out. I watch Zeb tending his bees, gardening, practicing martial arts.

Indoors I press random keys on our piano and thumb through books, reading their chapter titles and sentences.

Boots and I walk through the neighborhood. One day, we see Zeb patting dirt around his herb bed. He sees us head toward him and pulls something out of the ground and hands it to me, saying, "Basil, it chills you out."

I inhale. It is a wonderful scent that travels through my nose and throat before drifting in two directions—up into my head, down into my digestive tract. I look at Zeb, still squatting. His eyes are puffy. He is badly shaven. This man is suffering. I don't know what to say, but I want to communicate.

Warmth creeps through my chest, throat.

I feel concern, nausea.

"People think bees are angry, but bees are the opposite of that," he says.

But he does not explain what he means.

I put my hand on his shoulder for a long moment before I leave, walk home, clutching the herbs, feeling lubricated, porous, wary.

Boots and I return the next day. Zeb is in his backyard, playing guitar to a photograph of June that's hanging from a nail on the large tree he faces. I burst into tears. He keeps playing soft, pretty, and sad music, talking over it. I listen to and very much like these sounds but do not follow their content.

At some point, he puts his instrument down, says, "Hold on." He goes inside. He comes out with a fresh bowl of water. Puts it in front of Boots. He goes back inside and comes out with two tall glasses. Hands me one.

"Lemonade with basil. Did you try the stuff I gave you or just smell it? Basil is an underappreciated herb. Good for worry, good for appetite." We sit, sip.

He scans the scratches on my arms, bite marks on my wrists, my recklessly shaved head. Starts talking, saying something about how the word anger stems from the Old Norse word, grief. He keeps talking. I welcome the sound of his voice.

Anger and sadness. I believed I was helping June by declaring my allegiance through personal misery. But was I?

I look at her portrait, nailed to the tree, and face facts. How am I there for her? Or anyone—myself, my parents, Boots, Zeb, the bees, my friends. Do I have friends?

Zeb is still talking. I tune in when he says, "Moderate so you don't have to quit."

We sit in silence.

"Reign in that grief and fury, Elizabeth. Unchecked, they will surge, leaving you nothing but a binary choice: immersion or exit. Either way you lose grief potential, which you must consider as a great ally and weapon."

My body temperature rises.

Then he says, "You know that note your mom taped on your refrigerator, 'Everyone needs help from everyone'?"

Sort of. It has been on our refrigerator as long as I can remember, but I never think about it. I nod.

"Well," he says, "you are everyone."

I smile for the first time in a while. I also feel uncomfortably warm. Is this what people mean when they say stew? Don't people usually say "stew" when they brood angrily? I am not angry. In fact, I feel the opposite of anger. But my blood heads toward the boiling point.

How can I be everyone? Why am I interested in what Zeb says when I do not understand what he means?

He continues, "You know who said 'Everyone needs help from everyone'? Berthold Brecht. Your mom directed his plays back when she led that theater troupe."

I walk home. With each step, I am increasingly curious about mom's past.

But force myself to pack my questions up, put them into a cupboard, and lock the door. Because allowing myself to wonder too much about mom derails achieving my goal of solving this murder.

What I must do is cultivate heat brewing in my body.

The next morning I inaugurate a routine of private self-care: breath, piano, prayer.

Then browse through books and write down specific sentences in a journal June gave me, years ago, that sat unused in my dresser. The exercise brings multiple benefits. Engagement, focus and identifying connections between clues and sentences. Both are microcosms of potential. Both stand alone and with others. Sentences can construct a story or book. Clues can construct and solve a criminal case.

My morning sequence clears out space for observation. I notice ways sun streams through our windows. I see complex clumps of leaves and dirt on our garage floor and who comes through our neighborhood. How and when. This surveillance is practice. The perpetrator won't be back.

How do I know? I just do. Please do not mistake this for arrogance. There are many things inside me. Some are dull, naive, erroneous. Others, like buried treasure or unseen heroines, have value. Especially when they leave me and make their way out into the universe.

Back to sentence potency. I find a book on our shelf by Roberto Bolano titled "2666" and discover this line, "The sky, at sunset, looked like a carnivorous flower."

It's my introduction to a criminal profile.

Reading it, I know, hands down, that's them. That's June's killer.

I will recognize the killer when I see them.

Even if I do not yet understand why.

I need dad to talk through it.

Before June's murder, we took regular night walks. But that, like many routines, stopped after I found her dead. Now it's time we resume.

Isolation has its purpose and limitations. I want to engage more with the world but am not ready to plunge in. Walking with dad won't upset that balance.

I love him, it must be said. Moving together at night, through dark, empty streets, brainstorming, lubricates my thinking. So much has been gathered and stored since June's murder. I have to figure out what is worth keeping and what to tweak or obliterate.

I feel safe to free associate, safe to say meaningless, ill-informed, and partially valid things before landing on something solid.

Do things *mean* something if they stay inside you? Do they *mean* something if they don't?

I start our first new night-walk conversation with this line, "Without soul, a detective is nothing."

Dad asks where I heard that.

"You," I tell him.

He raises his eyebrows, shakes his head, says, "Well, I don't remember saying it. 'Without soul, a detective is nothing.' Hmmm. That is true morally but false practically. Some accomplished detectives are nasty pieces of work. Not unusual to find one who identifies the right perpetrator only to protect them. They gather evidence to convict and punish an innocent. Some might have a knack for something but use it in an ugly way. And even detectives who start off ok get twisted when they have to follow bad rules. They might begin their career incensed and over time get used to it. There are individual bad detectives and institutional ones. Anyway, so, yes. If I said that, it was a sugarcoat. As your father, I might have been rightly or wrongly, protective, and unsure how much truth you can handle."

"You never told me, I overheard you in conversation with Zeb," I say.

"Then I was joking. Or hoping," he says.

I amend the line: "Without soul, a detective is nothing. Nothing good."

See the power of a discrete sentence? Or two?

People don't always understand that an overheard line can make an impact. They mistake communication as something intentional, face to face, possibly scheduled, in a private room or across a table. But those times I, for one, zone out. Maybe because there is nothing for me to do but receive, and I function best when twining. Which means seeing and listening to random things not always, or ever, directed to me.

My goal—to solve June's case—keeps me in a specific lane. Anywhere outside of it, I lose the thread. I need this tight configuration, but I equally need to leave it, like when I brainstorm with dad.

Within boundaries.

This time, unlike our previous sessions, I do not want him brainstorming back. Because of my situational fragility. So when he riffs on things I say by disclosing innocent, even relevant personal thoughts like, "We all have to find places to live. For your mom, it is theater. For me, it is disrupting bureaucracy. For Zeb, it is music, and bees," I have no choice but to firmly divert him. When he talks about family history ("We had that theater for an explosive handful of years, then had you, Elizabeth. It just wasn't safe anymore, the kind of work we did.") I divert him, too.

These comments ruin my focus, and if I lose that, I blow it. By it I mean everything. In fact, his distractions raise my anxiety level so high that thoughts blur together in a frighteningly vague mass, and I fear the framework of this case I've been working so hard on will dissolve. Someday, I will want to learn about family history and elusive properties of guerrilla theater and how my birth impacted my parents. But not now. What I need now is tunnel vision.

So I distract him with the criminal profile line, "The sky, at sunset, looked like a carnivorous flower," and elaborate by explaining I found it looking through one of our books. Then detail why it is operational: It contains essential elements of the crime scene:

Place (sky)

Time (sunset)

Attribute, Victim (flower)

Attribute, Perpetrator (carnivorous flower)

I conclude, "Dad, I know there in those words I can find June's killer."

He puts his arm on my shoulder, says, "Ok."

June's case, my first, teaches the value of derailment. Time *away* allows me to spot information in Bolano's sentence that helps catch her killer. Early clues come (but pass unnoticed) months before the murder. During an after-school staff program called "Intro/Extro Version," I set up chairs, arrange drinks and snacks, so am allowed to stay for the documentary on the two profiles first identified by Swiss psychoanalyst Carl Jung in 1913 at the Fourth International Congress of Psychoanalysis in Munich.

Briefly:

You might see introverts crouch in corners, stare out windows, sit alone during breaks, but do not mistake this for bleak alienation. They tend to internally dialogue and may be meditating, dreaming, formulating strategies, songs, implementing projects.

You might see an extrovert in the center of a crowd talking, gesturing, basking in attention. Do not mistake this for superficiality. They think and listen best in public. Undaunted by failure, they flounder, fall, get up, go at it again, a persistence that attracts others. They expect, and appreciate, acknowledgement for achievements.

It can be a problem in each case if the behavior dominates the attribute—if isolation overrides the rich mental landscape of the introvert, if the need for adoration becomes negative attention seeking and overrides the bold extrovert's capabilities.

Each condition requires a specific response. Do not leave a sequestered introvert alone. Approach, but with care, the way you might a wounded bird or puppy. In contrast, do not approach a negative attention seeker. Rather watch, track, and assess. Then construct a strategy that draws them to you.

This information, from "Intro/Extro Version," resurfaces a while after June's death during an early morning breath, piano, prayer practice. When I remember it I re-read, "The sky, at sunset, looked like a carnivorous flower," and realize I already had the profile, but not the apprehension strategy. Now I see what it is. We are dealing with an extrovert so must draw them to us.

We do. Dad, Paula, and I do.

June. A part of me bristles at giving her killer any attention here. I want, instead, to think of June, ripped from this sphere, now living on only through stories. Here is not the place to share them. But I can mention her operatic voice, handcrafted briefcases, and silk skirts, memories that remind me to appreciate things here, now: Mom's woodwork and theater, Zeb's music and bees, Dad fighting his good fight, using, and subverting, bureaucracy.

Shouldn't I focus on these and other daily heroics, rather than her slayer and their bleak, sadistic, gesture?

Yet.

If we opened them up, what might we see? Landscapes, possibly ruined by mistreatment, like our oceans, jungles, and arctic circles are? Is it naïve, traitorous, and duplicitous to feel compassion, even love, for them? Not their act but them?

Maybe murderers vanish into the multi-sphere, are dismembered, and then rehabbed by cosmic forces.

Now, all these years later, I still present June's case professionally, citing Bolano's line as a classic criminal profile. Recently, a young officer in training raised her hand, recited a line from Shakespeare's *MacBeth* ("Look like the innocent flower/but be the serpent underneath"), and asked if that also described June's killer. The answer is No. Shakespeare's line is about theater, specifically playing a given role. It is an excellent directive for agents working undercover. Bolano's profile, in contrast, has nothing to do with play-acting. His line expresses something deep down to the bone and tendons. It references an essential coordinate of someone, or a portion of someone, who lives to cultivate and display a specific brand of malevolence, someone who lays their cards for us face up on the table. There is nothing covert or performative about it.

But I assured her the question is excellent, and shows how much words matter.

Personal process. My thoughts are chaotic and stuck in one place, me. I spend a *lot* of time considering what to hone, direct, and release, being careful not to aggressively purge.

Swinging between extremes—hope, despair—while working a case, fuels me. One, then the other, then the one. Hope fills me with radiance, lifts me up toward the stars. Despair enters, grounds me. Hope, then, swoops me upward again. I'm powered by hope, but once astral, I lose touch with humanity. To reconnect, I drop down. Being earthbound nourishes, just to a point, then stagnates, creeps toward sadness, despondency. Which is when I again surge upward, resisting the urge to stay airborne and fuse with the sky.

These two extremes, in the right amounts, generate a momentum that fuels productivity in my personal practice. It is the only way I can do it. By "it," I mean everything. Not that I solve each case.

But I do give each one my all. And for that discrete period, I am in service of things strong, strange, and beautiful.

Do not mistake my process as instruction. When it comes to style, I find, and employ, mine. You, find, then employ, yours. Without that we are nothing. Well, no, not nothing. But we are diminished.

10 Lines of Duty

Agent Bruno

My daughter, Elizabeth, a fine detective, puts herself in training right from the start when she, an untrained teenager, profiles a killer from a book sentence and helps apprehend him with strategy learned from a school documentary about intro- and extroversion. I hoped she would move on from tracking murder to some form of bureaucratic forensics because I hated thinking of her dealing with all that savagery.

"They fuck you up, your mum and dad," said some Brit. Now, frustratingly, here I am, a dad, doing it. But I catch myself doing it and say, "Bruno, stop. It is you, not your daughter, who cringes at violence. Don't conflate."

The blurred boundaries might come from having a child later in life. Later in life as a considered decision, not a careless act of intimacy. Later in life when you are employed, partnered, and a homeowner. When you are dedicated to raising your desired child right, therefore must dismantle and restructure established patterns and boundaries around things that served and still serve you. Things like working, thinking, jogging, hanging out, and having sex. The adjustment is a drag. But you get used to it. In fact, you come to relish it. You soon find your best life with this child who you love and who loves you. There is so much to live and be thankful for.

Then she reaches an age when she does not need or want your brand of steady care. In fact, she finds it and you annoying. Questions and comments that used to be answered with a "Yes," an "Ok," or a hand clap ("More toast?", "Wear a sweater!", "Want to play catch?") now get a "No" or an eye roll.

My wife, Elizabeth's mother, Hanna, unsurprisingly has no problem with the transition or with transitions in general. She adopts a role and then shifts to another, all the while staying herself. Yes she is an actress. But, more importantly, owns a solid center and is able to reallocate offshoots of routines and affection without diminishment. Think of a longstanding tree. Hanna is its multiple, blossoming branches. I am the trunk, inching slowly in one simple vertical direction. It's just me who has problems with change in our family. As Elizabeth matures and I get personal time and privacy back, I struggle to make them great again. So I soul search, and over time, with Paula's help, I discover how to update myself, and my father/daughter bond, at once: detective work.

I don't track or even help track individual killers because the immediacy of violence is too brutal for me personally. I fall for tragic scenarios around murders and missing persons. I imagine—to the point where I partially feel—the anguish of the target and their loved ones. I graphically picture the victim days, hours, and moments leading up to the attack. I see their lifeless body the instant after. I envision kidnapped people quivering, bound, drugged, starved, routinely assaulted. The friends and family grappling with the disappearance, wondering if the absent one has done a runner, collapsed from an illness, maybe eloped or is planning a surprise. Then, as time drags on and such possibilities seem uncertain, I can imagine these friends and family members sitting or pacing inside public halls, private living rooms, stunned, sickened, terrified. Or outdoors recklessly stomping, searching, hoping to help or at least have something to do. My internal narratives around these scenes are pictorial, detailed, and invasive.

Elizabeth, in contrast, compartmentalizes. She takes on grizzly case elements with a determination to consider and solve. She dissects and analyzes motive, strategy, background and their intersection. Her profiles help officers identify and apprehend elusive nasties: the methodic carnival worker, the petulant industrialist, the cocky college student, the bored entrepreneur convinced they are underappreciated.

Not my lane.

My daughter and I work in crime but have different job sets. She focuses on individuals, while I fixate on structures. My colleagues and I address small pieces of this wreckage when we can by employing process and technology to investigate misdoings of fake legitimates—meaning, legal government and corporate systems built on narrowly specific values turned into rules, manuals, and laws. In other words, bogus truths. Our target is not a discrete human but an apparatus: broad, deep, multi-tentacled. Our marks are wealthy companies that wreak widescale damage yet *contribute*. For example, they authorize toxic dumps in waterways *and* launch and fund charitable and arts foundations. They evade taxes *and* employ people and provide them with insurance, resumes, security, and upward mobility.

Think of Elizabeth's approach as a spear, ours as seepage. In June's case, they intersect. The murderer Elizabeth profiles and helps apprehend is embedded within and protected by a vast entity and its well-padded, protected branches.

We have a book in our home library that has "banality of evil" in its title. The three words profile a large portion of my criminal targets—like legal organizations that task workers to authorize damaging procedures with a click or a signature without making clear where they lead. For example, the staff is assigned daily tasks (signing a form, sending an invoice) that can and do land them in positions of inflicting harm without intending to: okaying the previously mentioned dumped waste and other things like a signature that (not obviously) okays animal overcrowding in food factories and diminishes pension plans. Or an order to employ staff from a national roster, not the communities the companies are based in. Or a form that mandates staff below a certain wage level park far off site and must shuttle to the office.

Workers executing a discrete duty rather than an intentional cruelty. It is not a murder or an assault but compliance with job duties.

This is how I understand, and am helped professionally by the term "banality of evil." Harm done within a social and legal contract. Not slitting a throat or bombing a bank or breaking the leg of a racehorse. I have not read the book or even ever removed it from our shelf. My take on its partial title may or may not be faithful to the author's intent, but it serves me personally and professionally, so I stick with it. I could say bureaucracies are the real evil, not killers. But the fact is they are both bad. My job is with systems because of my skill set.

Process

You might see me working, hunched over my desk, tapping its surface, rubbing my scalp and chin, missing cigarettes. I love my job but might not appear to. I thrive on worry and anxiety. My cases bring both. I would not have it any other way. I sit as long as possible because breaks interrupt my thought train. For maximum productivity, I need to be patient and never expect consistent momentum. Like my favorite off duty activity, fishing, I don't do it for consistent, immediate results. Some days I catch fish. Some days I don't. I am happy to provide these work details and any documentation of my successes and failures. I am unhappy with visual documentation of me physically at work, especially by a stranger. How I look is not representative of who I am, how I think, or what I do. When I work, I look miserable but feel electric. In contrast, Elizabeth appears serene but tells me she does not feel that way. She sits in an erect half lotus and pours over notes, files, and documents between moments of stillness—eyes closed or maybe staring into space. Yet she tells me she feels intense anxiety. She hides it while working. When it creeps in, she has outlets. Job stress fuels her to move away from one spot to others: books, piano, yards, people. For example, she walks Boots, converses with Zeb, and returns to a case sharing something he said, like "Honeybees like white clover but not red clover because their tongues are too short to reach the nectar" and regains her composure. When I hear Zeb say things like that, I ruminate on them all day. So I wait till evening or weekends to spend time with him. He diverts me from work but gives me pleasure off hours. But for Elizabeth, this is not a diversion but a switch that opens a door to a case breakthrough. "Breaks," she says, "clear my thinking because they help soften the enormity of it all."

Why do the powerful and the privileged usually feel the most beleaguered? I don't know, but I do know they do. June's killer is an example. Influential, infatuated (with multiple intense short lived interests), convinced of his long personal sufferance. I debated disclosing his name here. But omission is unusual and will draw attention. Standing out in any way is the first thing he wants and the last thing he needs, so I have no problem stating his name: George. Think of all the good Georges: Carlin, Clinton, Gershwin and, the great British detective, Gently. June's killer, George, will never ruin the name. So from here on, George. If hate is a thing, I feel it for him. But I do not want to stoop that low. So when I sense the sentiment seeping in, I breathe deeply and mentally repeat: *Be the change, Bruno.*

George. The CEO ruining our municipal river by ordering executives to task staff with signing forms that allow it to be filled with poisonous chemicals. June, an environmental lawyer, makes a case to halt this, and—because this does not happen—close the factory.

The company counters with an airtight legal defense.

June finds a loophole.

Her win, his/their loss took George to a new place.

Until then, I did not fully understand the precision of Elizabeth's profile ("The sky at sunset looked like a carnivorous flower") but once I saw him interviewed, I understood completely. It is not just his profile but his plan. He murdered June at sunset and in his mind transitioned her to the sky.

Elizabeth and I watch footage of our investigator interviewing George in his office. George presents himself like the educated contemporary he is. Tall, limber, white shirt and teeth, colorful embroidered wristbands, Bermudas (we first met in summer), tanned shins. He quotes the same Nietzsche line twice: "The higher we soar the smaller we appear to those who cannot fly." In his office, he has pictures of himself doing arm balances in busy markets and in front of a temple in Mumbai because he likes to travel. Because he feels that India is home. Because, there, he got off prescribed pharmaceuticals. Because India feeds his soul and reminds him to meditate, pray, and eat vegetarian. Because it reminds him he is privileged and must give back.

After the self disclosure, he explains that June was wrong to shut his company down. His dumping was legal. He owns the land and the building and is allowed access to adjacent water. He gives back. His chicken feeds families. June's actions were wrong, but she was giving him a flirt. His face softens, his eyes grow misty, and he gives a small smile as he veers into a story about June. About the first time he saw her. About how in her he met his match. A match for another, not this, dimension. How they can and will co-exist in the sky. How she orchestrated her murder. To expedite it, she pretended to go against him. Her dissent made it impossible for them to be together in this here, now, but opened the door for their muti-spheric future. How they were both at a point where they need someone or thing to tell them what to do. She asked for her "murder," an end to one phase that paves the way to another. Where they will hold hands, leap over oceans, islands and continents. Her death here, in this dimension, is the first step toward their infinite union in others. The plan gave him something bigger than this time and place to think about. Something greater. Another life, one of beauty, meaning, embellishment. He details how he searched long and hard for that substantial pin to fasten his note to her silk skirt. He bought it at an antique shop in Italy. He details how he thought so deeply about his note, choosing words from, Leonard Cohen's "Hallelujah" ("But you don't really care for music, do you?") and the gothic font he used to pen it. For that period, he expressed himself in a way that was truly and distinctly him. No one else could do what he did the way he did it. That image of her, dead, radiating beauty, eliciting pity. Her murder was his love letter. It will take him and June to a new place. They share a deep love for music. They will be soon, somewhere, with music, together. And islands. And trees. And they will be able to fly. How meeting June, her beating him, then him beating her, opened the door for them to be together always. In solidarity.

Listening to this puts us in a sickening position. We have to let him talk. But this kind of speech feeds something terrible. A bleak, gaping vanity. It does not get us closer to what we need. In fact, it distances us from our goal. We are invested in solving this case. June was our friend, our neighbor. Hearing this use of words—evil from the mouth of a criminal who is self-congratulating—means we must shut him down. He is padding. We need an effective intervention.

Elizabeth did it. "I found June, I will take this," she said, then stood up, entered the room, sat next to the interviewer, across from George. She asked him to repeat his story. He, visibly pleased to have a new audience, readily talked. He talked at length, settling more and more deeply into his chair. She did not need to continue questioning. Our interviewer covered that. She needed to disrupt. At some point Elizabeth opened her folder, took out a piece of paper with a pre-prepared, neatly typed sentence and handed it to him and said, "George, can you please read this to us?" He took the paper and read, "The truth and the whole truth are not the same thing." Then looked at Elizabeth. She asked him to read it again. And again. He did, and grew increasingly derailed. Because of the power shift. Because it prevented him from using his own words and cornered him into speaking responsibly.

Paula taught us that with perpetrators like him, you appeal to their vanity then pull the advantage away. George started nodding while reciting the line, sensing his vanity was being rewarded with power. But then he slowed down and stopped talking. His eyes settled into a blank pool. He appeared emotionless like a primordial shark or serpent. The words outwitted him, therefore shut him down. Nothing stops people who *believe* they are truly intelligent more than something that truly is. "The truth and the whole truth are not the same thing."

Elizabeth leaned toward him, "Don't misunderstand me. We don't doubt your connection to everything you've told us. But it is your clipped version. We have a bigger, more comprehensive version. One that, along with our data, proves your truth and the whole truth aren't the same thing. You, George, are heading to jail, not the sky."

This was the first, but not last, case my daughter and I worked on together.

Elizabeth's profile identified George. Her apprehension strategy caught him. My team's forensics gathered necessary prosecuting data and closed the factory.

My daughter and I are dedicated professionals with, as Paula helped us see, complementary but different skill sets. This case, June's, is our first but not last. We do not always team up but when we do it is a privilege. And effective.

11 The Angels & Me

Paula

When people ask if I incorporate angels into my crime fighting career I answer, *sometimes.*

Then I tell a story.

Here is one:

Our neighbor opens the family basement to her young son, Jeb, and friends so they can engage and expend energy within the contained space. She names it Fort, after her childhood treehouse. It's a tribute to the unsupervised, often happy, ultimately bittersweet hours spent there. Fresh air and freedom led to some trouble, resulting in her father tearing the place down, which is why she gives her son a basement, not a treehouse. The boys meet for years and are in high school when this story takes place.

Fort has posters, a record player, comics, a refrigerator, a taxidermied deer bust and wall of resin-encased bugs. Its separate entrance does not lead into the home, proper. Now, instead of Legos, holsters, and Tinkertoys, boys bring guitars, amplifiers, and weed.

I hang out there, the only girl, welcomed because I wear lipstick and ignore them. What do I get from Fort? Peace. I have problems with mental focus. Only there can I lose myself. At this time it is in a book, *Our Mutual Friend,* by Charles Dickens—mostly because of his character Eugene Wrayburn. Witty, flawed, physically frail, ultimately redeemable. "'I hate,' said Eugene, putting his legs up on the opposite seat, 'I hate my profession.'"

He is a lawyer.

The boys listen to and play music, get high, and banter. I read and think. Fort gives us all space to do what we want. It makes school days endurable.

Then.

Jeb's *uncle* comes to town, boarding temporarily with the family. He hangs out in Fort, radiates helplessness. His appearance is disheveled. Dirty yellow jacket, thick glasses, poor posture, heavy gait. Minimal eye contact. The boys don't register his presence, but I do. Periodically, I put down my book and ask if he wants something to eat or drink.

So it is a shock when, one evening, walking home from piano, I see him standing in an alley, changing clothes. His glasses, jeans, and smudged yellow jacket go into a duffel. On go track pants and a formfitting shirt. His eyes, I can see from a distance, well, with binoculars, are penetrating blue. He moves like a panther. He is a liar. My pity turns to thrill. Attraction.

For now, all I will say, because this is a whole other story, is one thing leads to another: he harms me and leaves me for dead.

But I don't die. Thanks to angels, I survive.

And for a long period it is in a temporary border state.

I am partly in a hospital bed, on life support. Partly airborne, disembodied. I see but am not seen. There is *poetry to the invisible* but practicality as well. Especially when mixed with the power of action.

Initially I want to inflict harm on this uncle. Push him into traffic, stab his eyes, lop off a hand. But the angels intervene. They shepherd me back in time. We visit his childhood, and when I see the things done to him, my heart breaks. I want to cradle this small boy in my arms, take him to safety. I'd gladly trade my life for his if there could be a way to keep him from the inflicted damage. But that is not possible. Feelings of revenge melt into a wide open heart, momentarily unprotected. But the angels force me to face what I want to ignore: that was then, this is now. Excessive childhood mistreatment constructed a nasty adult. He leaves a victim trail. I am not the first and won't be the last.

The reality check turns my lens to justice.

As much as I want to kill, I strategize instead.

I sweep into my home, get a baggie from the kitchen, and grab my high school photo ID and a monogrammed charm bracelet from my dresser. Then I fly to the hospital. I see myself pale, barely breathing, hooked up to machines, and cut a lock of my hair and add it to the baggie. By now school is getting out. I hover over our neighborhood until I see him heading *home,* swoop down, insert my package into his pocket. Then get to the top of Fort's stairs and wait. I hear the boys. I know they talk about me, but I do not want to listen. At this moment I am one-hundred-percent mission driven. When he enters, as I know he will, I trip him. He topples downstairs. The boys call an ambulance that takes him to the hospital. During his treatment process, my planted evidence is found. He is apprehended, subjected to the wheels of "justice."

I worry.

Not about him but me. About my lack of emotional judgment. It tells me I might have a knack for espionage, but I do not work well unsupervised. If I have any hope to continue in this line of work, I need guidance and for now it is these angels.

Guest Lecture Series: Performance

Dr. Natambu

Trust is critical for agent performance, but long-term loyalty is impossible to regulate. Espionage is not linear. Agents must understand when to follow, reject, break, or bend (that is, *creatively utilize*) procedure. Strategically fluid rule navigation allows for degrees of discreet infraction, which can help crack a case or lead to gradual, initially unintended betrayal. Effective course plotting combined with advice and personally gleaned information and solid spiritual practice help keep detection honest but no measures are foolproof.

Secret intelligence and corruption go together but not inevitably. Secret intelligence and lying, in contrast, are inextricably linked. We will come to that momentarily. For now, let's consider three common corruption triggers: greed, empathy, and their intersection.

Personal greed is perhaps the best known and covered reason for deceit. Depictions of bent agents rubbing elbows with, even joining, the very rich (enjoying their cars, clubs, drugs, escorts, parties on private planes, boats, and islands) are well-documented in books, films, and news reports.

We mentioned empathic defection. In this case, agents graft assets for unselfish, even compassionate, reasons. Especially when operating undercover.

Most agencies deal with two forms of detection: abstract and covert. The first, which is not our focus today, tracks individual and group activity with hidden cameras, recording equipment, wiretapping, and cyber monitoring. Because information is amassed and tracked impersonally, case decisions are based on data, not human interaction. Consequences (arrests, rescues, removals, raids, attacks) are therefore easier, from an emotional standpoint, to implement aggressively. None of this applies, of course, if the enforcer is a psychopath, but we weed that profile out of our selection process. Or try to.

Undercover detection, in contrast, involves interface. Information is gathered through varying degrees of personal dealings. Our undercover agents infiltrate the life of a person, family, or community to gain enough material to solve or stop criminal activity—such as weapon smuggling, drug production and distribution, or sex trafficking.

Sometimes we recruit and train people who are possibly indigenous to the targeted sector. They, therefore, deal with those they grew up with and with whom they share community, customs, history and values. These *homegrown* agents rarely work alone but usually together with implanted external professionals.

Both sets are trained in basics. They compile information, hone instincts, navigate rules, stay on a target's tail, attack others and protect themselves. They withstand extreme temperatures, sensory deprivation, mock executions and other more extreme forms of torture.

The local employee already has links but must learn different and arguably more sensitive and ethically thorny forms of duplicity than the outsiders. They lie to people they know and perhaps depend on. They lie to those they love.

Our external undercovers, in contrast, train to gain detailed familiarity with the culture being permeated and the individuals within it. Their access vehicle is a carefully selected persona. It could be a phantom (ghostlike, intentionally invisible, or at least of no interest to, to targets) or a vivid character—like a singer, gardener, janitor, housekeeper, passerby, cyclist, teacher, artist, waitress, neighbor, interior designer, or baker. Both kinds of agents require performance skills. Performance is, hands down, the most crucial element of successful undercover work. If a disguise is blown, our mission, our agents, and innocents are all at risk. Individuals, families, communities, entire countries can be set back because of one single blown cover. A skilled agent must be a skilled actor. If they flounder, they can die. People they try to protect can die. Our mission can die.

We enlist classically-trained dramatists to coach our agents. Agents do not go into the field before mastering drama basics (intonation, carriage, eye movement) and consistently adhering to characters' clothing, food and beverage choices, and their work and hobbies. Above all, agents hone the ability to improvise. Undercover work is impossible to script.

So far so good. Now let's look at a performance shift that imperils any mission: when an agent's *role* becomes *real*.

How does this happen? Emotions.

Sometimes a slip is done for a professionally indefensible reason: a *ghost* becomes a stalker, a *housekeeper* steals jewelry, a *teacher* crosses an intimacy line with a student. But more often the infraction is motivated by feelings—or what our agents imagine are their feelings—that enrich any society: empathy, concern, and, it must be said, love.

An example of compassion-driven, finance-based, mission betrayal: grafted resources go not in an agent's personal account but toward supplying an individual, family, or entire neighborhood with clean water, medical care, extra protection, or relocation to safety.

Then there are the more personal but not ill-intended slips. A *cyclist* grows enamored with the landscape and then, discovering pollutants with various degrees of toxicity, worries about its birds, ferns, and insects—in short, the landscape's future—and *therefore* focuses on ecological activism, not professional duties. A *singer*, heartbroken by social program cuts, decides to pursue a lucrative show business career, amass a fortune, and donate it all to struggling charities. A *waitress* makes an inroad with a bar owner who allows child porn to be filmed in the basement and is unnerved enough to assault him with a bat and toilet plunger.

All true, not anecdotal, examples.

To stay tethered to a mission, agents must perform and remind themselves that they are performing. Their job is to play a role, not function authentically. They must—to use a term from object relations theory in psychoanalytic psychology—split. Between the self and the role. Otherwise things get personally twisted. The mission crashes, burns, implodes. We train agents to sense such oncoming slippage and seek help. Once we know, we have methods to arrest the process.

Splitting, like many qualities necessary for good espionage, leads to extreme dysfunction *on the outside*. Agents who actually slip into *healthy for the outside* states (like blending love and work; experiencing tenderness in spiritual, friendly or romantic ways; telling the truth to friends, colleagues, family members) are a consistent, perilous, bureau threat. We call this shift—when the *role* becomes *real*—empathic infidelity.

Undercover work means faking honesty. It means lying and possibly betraying someone or thing no matter what. There is no getting around it. If our people form a true allegiance with infiltrated mission communities, then they damage agency performance. Remaining loyal to us at the bureau means they deceive and likely damage the target population.

We have faith in philanthropic espionage. Yet there is no getting around the fact all operations do, to varying degrees, put innocents in danger. Yet we value the higher purpose enough to condone degrees of strategic deceit. This point, understandably debatable, will be examined in a later lecture.

Philanthropic espionage. We believe it can exist. Even though it currently does not. We make a decision to acknowledge its potential. We don't quit just because we are not there. We move toward there. We look at what we are, and at what we can be. As an agency, we achieve mission accomplishment but strive to do better when it comes to altruism. We are proud of the first. As for the second, we accept, for now, a sentiment from the great Austrian writer Thomas Bernhard: "After all, there is nothing but failure."

For Now.

Key

Names of artists and spaces that launched each piece

Agency Overview (Hoss) Peter Williams

1. **Personal Practice (Paula)** Peter Williams
2. **Dawnstorm (Agent Jennifer)** Marie T. Hermann
3. **TNW & Me (Effie)** Peter Williams
4. **The Spy Who Hung Out in the Cold (To: Chief Hoss From: Paula Regossy Item: Journalistic Art Document)** MBad African Bead Museum (Olayami Dabls), Detroit Institute of Arts (Diego Rivera, Caravaggio, Elizabeth Murray), Youngworld (Jeremy Couillard, Claire Ashley, Lan Touzon)
5. **Dose (Paula/Eva)** Nancy Mitchnik
6. **Staredown (Agent Joan)** Chido Johnson
7. **Difference not Value (Agent Jos)** John Corbin, Osman Khan, Peter Markus
8. **Same Sky (Agent Nadea)** Addie Langford, Neha Vetpathak

9 &10. **Lines of Duty (Agent Elizabeth)** and **Lines of Duty (Agent Bruno)** Biba Bell, Carole Harris, Maya Stovall

11. **The Angels & Me (Paula)** Claire Ashley, Jim Chatelain

Guest Lecture Series: Performance (Dr. Natambu) Anthony Marcellini, Cezanne Charles

Acknowledgments

This book began with a painting, *Pussy Galore,* by Peter Williams, I first saw at Paul Kotula Projects in Ferndale, Michigan. Because this character came from a James Bond film, I got the idea to write a spy novel with a heroine named Paula Regossy, which is an anagram of "Pussy Galore." I did not stop there. Each chapter in this book is my personal (but faithful) response to works by various Detroit-based artists and spaces. I converse with, ruminate on, and scrutinize the work and/or the venue before I construct the narratives. *Paula Regossy* would not exist without these people, works, and places.

The author would like to thank the following Detroit locations: Cranbrook Art Museum (Bloomfield Hills), Detroit Institute of Arts, Hill Gallery (Birmingham), Lafayette Towers, MBad African Bead Museum, Museum of Contemporary Art Detroit, N'Namdi Center for Contemporary Art, Paul Kotula Projects (Ferndale), Simone DeSousa Gallery, and Youngworld. The author would also like to thank the Robert Rauschenberg Foundation, and the following publications in which some of these texts previously appeared: *Big Other; Detroit Research; Fence; Infinite Mile; Kumusha II: Between Two Rocks (Zimbabwe-Detroit); Nancy Mitchnik: Uncalibrated,* (Museum of Contemporary Art Detroit); and *The N-Word* (Rotland Press).

Opening quote from *Bulletproof Diva: Tales of Race, Sex and Hair* by Lisa Jones (Anchor, 1997)

Trinosophes is a multidisciplinary art space in Detroit, Michigan, presenting concerts, exhibitions, film screenings, and literary events by international and local artists. The venue is also the publisher of the artist-run record label, Two Rooms Records, as well as Trinosophes Editions.